DEVIL'S END

A MASON NASH NOVEL

DAVE SINCLAIR

ALSO BY DAVE SINCLAIR

Mason Nash Novels

Past Transgressions

Shadow Hunting

Devil's End

Atticus Wolfe Novels

Out of Time

It Takes a Spy

The Coldest War

Charles Bishop Novels

Kiss My Assassin

Agent Provocateur

Venetian Blonde

Eva Destruction Novels

The Barista's Guide to Espionage

The Rookie's Guide to Espionage (novella)

The Amnesiac's Guide to Espionage

The Dead Spy's Guide to Espionage

For Piers Morton.
*My old housemate who, after one too many sessions of me
complaining about some piece of writing, said the words, "Well,
why don't you try and do better?"*
*That little phrase put me on my long journey as a writer.
What a bastard.*

ONE

Nash had to concede that for the first time in his life, he was fully content.

Not just happiness, but true contentment. Happiness is fleeting and generated by external factors based on emotion, whereas contentment is a state of mind. Happiness is a reaction; contentment is a lasting calmness. And it had indeed lasted. In the five weeks he'd been in Nepal, Nash had experienced a peace he'd never known before.

It was the state he'd hoped to achieve after he'd retired from MI6 and moved to the English countryside but had never quite attained, in spite of all the yoga and meditation. It had taken total isolation in this far-flung little town to reach this higher level of inner peace.

Meandering down a dirt track beside a small creek, he was in no particular rush. None of the friendly locals he passed appeared to be either. The occasional dog would amble up for a scratch behind the ear and then wander off to find some shade from the midday sun.

Panauti was thirty kilometres southeast of Kathmandu.

Nash was staying with a lovely local family in their guest house, as there were no nearby hotels. It cost him the equivalent of six pounds a night including meals, which was fortunate, as there were no restaurants to speak of.

Nash was living his idyllic life. He only wished he could stay, but knew he couldn't—for so many reasons.

Dressed in the local garb of a linen kurta and three-quarter pants, Nash slowly made his way to the old part of the city with its forty-odd temples. Panauti was laid back and unhurried and nowhere near as busy as the touristy Kathmandu or Bhaktapur. There was hardly any traffic on the patchy roads, and despite being the only Westerner, no one had tried to sell him anything.

Part of the reason Nash was here was to heal, mentally and physically. It had taken weeks for his body to recover from recent incidents, longer still for his mind to start to mend. No matter how comfortable and at peace he was, there was always a splinter in his mind, the reminder that his work was not yet done. There was one task only Nash could complete.

He had to bring down Tartarus.

The evil private spy agency had grown even stronger, more powerful, more ambitious. It had killed hundreds of innocents, manipulated world governments and framed Nash and his friends for the worst of it. Former MI6 espionage agents Nash, Eva Destruction, Charles Bishop and Paul Cavendish were now the most wanted ex-spies on the planet. Every major government was on the lookout for them while the heads of Tartarus only strengthened their grip on power, moving ever closer to legitimacy and acceptance by those they wished to overthrow.

Despite appearances, Nash wasn't hiding, he was biding his time. Tartarus had their people embedded in every major espionage agency and would be scouring every corner of the globe for Nash and his team. Even with the combined spy networks of the legitimate secret service organisations, they would be hard-pressed to find him in Panauti. They might be good, but he doubted any were *that* good; although the Himalayan sheepdog nearby was eying him suspiciously. He gave pooch a belly rub and sent him on his way, hoping he'd keep Nash's secret.

Tartarus were still out there, somewhere, but for Nash to take them on he needed to be whole again; Nepal had given him that. Part of him, a large part, wanted to stay, to ignore the rest of the world and its frivolous global politics and endless wars and just *be*. But as strong as the pull was, Nash knew deep down he could never stay, not until his role in the story was done. His moral core could never allow that level of malevolence to win. No, this tranquillity he felt was only fleeting. He couldn't stay, not until Tartarus's house of lies had been burnt to the ground. But there would be no burning today. He had temples to investigate.

Reaching the old town, Nash took time to admire the traditional Newa architecture. He waved to the local children, who felt comfortable saying hello to the man with the unruly grey beard who had been in their midst for weeks and didn't seem to be going anywhere.

Today's trek took him to the Indreshwar Mahadev Temple, which was over seven hundred years old. Dedicated to Shiva, it was Panauti's oldest and most beloved temple. Nash had deliberately left this pagoda as his last to explore. His thinking was that you don't start a meal with dessert, you finish strong. This would be his last temple before he left his little isolation bubble for the real world. He wanted to make it count.

Various smaller monuments surrounded the main

temple. Stone lions guarded each of the entrances. Several puja, or shrines, containing offerings were scattered around the temple.

Nash slowly circled the ground level, where two small doors were surrounded by round panels with high blind windows positioned near the corners. Roof struts depicted various goddesses, some in sensuous poses. It was a breath-taking building. Using his digital SLR, Nash snapped photos from various angles. Soon, that wasn't all he was taking photos of.

Over the last few weeks Nash had learned to identify the locals on sight; their mannerisms, their habits. While he didn't speak the local dialect, a friendly wave or mimes to induce a laugh had endeared him to most. The locals seemed to like the strange tall man in their midst. Nash could spot a tourist miles away. He chuckled to himself. *Tourist.* He was even beginning to think like a local.

The three newcomers arrived at the same time Nash did. Two women and a man. Under the pretext of photographing the temple, Nash surreptitiously took pictures of each of them. Entering the temple alone, he zoomed in on the images to confirm his suspicions.

By the time tourists reached Panauti they were well and truly dishevelled. No one started a holiday in a town this far from civilisation. It was only the most ardent and dedicated long-term travellers who came this far off the beaten track. So why, then, were these tourists' backpacks and clothing brand new? Why were their fingernails so clean, their hiking boots straight out of the box and the man clean shaven?

There was a simple explanation: they weren't tourists.
They've found me.

In an instant, all of Nash's contentment was washed

away by the firehose of reality, leaving behind a square-jawed professional. He placed his hemp bag and camera quietly on the wooden floor and did his best to mentally prepare for what was to come. He cracked his neck and stepped outside.

From their facial features, the three were likely of Chinese heritage, though that was hardly a definitive gauge of nationality. All did their best to cast their eyes in any direction but his.

Shoddy spycraft, guys.

Most people took at least a fraction of a second to glance at anyone exiting a temple. Not these three. They were careful to ensure they didn't gaze at Nash at all, even though he was the only white guy for kilometres. A reliable sign they were, in fact, shadowing him. To be visible like this, they were either arrogant, or had enough backup to ensure they could be.

Throughout Nash's long career he'd learned that sometimes the best form of defence was attack. Equally, he'd learned that sometimes, it was running away. And yet at other times, defence was best served by completely confusing your enemy.

He quite liked the latter.

Stepping towards the non-tourists, he waved a friendly hand. "Hey there, I'm Mason Nash. I believe you're looking for me, as I'm wanted by... well, everyone."

The three stared at him in stunned silence. Coloured prayer flags fluttered in the wind.

There was surely nothing in their handbook for this eventuality. How to strangle a man? Sure. Countersurveillance in a built-up area? Undoubtedly. What to do when your surveillance target identifies themselves and walks over to you with a big stupid grin? Unlikely.

They all gawped at him, shocked. But not shocked enough to keep them from reaching for their very un-tourist-like Chinese manufactured QSZ-92 pistols and pointing them at Nash.

"You're... giving yourself up?" the male asked.

His accent was thick. English wasn't his native language.

Nash stepped close to the man. The two women sensibly remained close, but out of striking distance.

Still grinning, Nash replied, "Well, I don't know about giving myself up, per se. Perhaps we could have a little chat and see where things lead, hmm?"

Confusion crinkled the man's forehead. "You've admitted you are the criminal, Mason Nash."

"I admitted the latter, not the former. That's all Tartarus propaganda."

"What's a Tartarus?"

That one took Nash by surprise. "So... you're not Tartarus?"

The man shook his head in genuine confusion. "My name's Feng."

"No, I mean who do you work for?"

"I work for State Security Ministry."

So, they were Chinese secret service. The organisation was the principal civilian intelligence, security and secret police agency of the People's Republic of China. No slouches in the world of espionage. One should never underestimate them.

Nash's eyes narrowed. "Who do you *really* work for?"

"Mr Zang?"

"And who's he then?"

"My supervisor at the Ministry." Feng scratched the back of head but made sure the QSZ-92 didn't stray from

Nash. "Look, I'm going to be honest here, I'm a bit lost with this whole conversation."

"You and me both, buddy." Nash planted his fists on his hips. "You're telling me you've never heard of Tartarus?"

"Is that a sports drink?"

In retrospect, assuming they were Tartarus was unrealistic. Tartarus were good, very good, but even they couldn't be in all places at once. That was part of the reason Nash and his compatriots had been framed for Tartarus's crimes: so legitimate spy agencies could do Tartarus's dirty work for them.

None of them had even flinched when he'd mentioned Tartarus. The organisation wasn't all-powerful just yet. Although they'd infiltrated every major spy agency, not all spies in the world were on their payroll. It was conceivable these three weren't Tartarus at all, just sent to investigate a vague lead about an unidentified bearded man in an out-of-the-way place. They likely had many such innocuous leads to follow up, it just so happened these three had been sent after the real Mason Nash. If it were a simple lead follow-up, that likely meant there wouldn't be backup or legions of Chinese spies about to descend on the temple complex. To Nash, that may be the only glimmer of hope in this whole situation.

If these three weren't connected to Tartarus, that meant they were just doing their job, and Nash wished them no ill will. Although he wasn't sure that sentiment would be reflected back.

He held up his hands. "I don't want a fight. I'm a pacifist and don't wish to harm anyone."

The taller female frowned. "I've seen your file. You're no more a pacifist than I am a hamster." Her English was flawless.

Nash pinged her as the lead of the operation. "I've changed."

Feng stepped forward and thrust his gun in Nash's face. "On the ground, now!"

Driven by pure instinct, Nash reacted. Taking a confident stride forward, his lightning-fast hands grasped the pistol and twisted it painfully away from Feng. His right hand dug into his opponent's palm, peeling the weapon from his grasp. Once in his possession, Nash ejected the cartridge and peeled back the slide to eject the bullet in the barrel then dropped the weapon, holding his hands up in surprise. It was a motor reflex reaction that took all of a second and a half.

Apparently unimpressed with Nash's disarming skills, the now unarmed Feng screeched in anger. He lunged forward, throwing a telegraphed right fist at Nash. Side-stepping it neatly, Nash let Feng's forward momentum carry him past then, utilising the man's off kilter mass, grasped the back of his head and introduced his face to Nash's knee. The loud crack told him they had been suitably acquainted. With Feng still on his feet, Nash grabbed the back of his jacket and bum rushed him headfirst into a nearby offering shrine, sending incense, flowers and fruit flying.

Standing legs akimbo, Nash held his palms up, doing his best to appear as unthreatening to the two remaining Chinese agents as possible. He suspected the gesture was unsuccessful.

The lead female raised her pistol to Nash's head but remained a respectable distance away. "Changed, have you?" She flicked a thumb towards her subordinate. "His broken nose says otherwise."

"The fact that he's still breathing is evidence enough."

Nash sighed. "Believe it or not, I don't wish to hurt anyone. I made a vow that wherever possible I will inflict no harm, try to make up for the life you read about in my file. And as comprehensive as it is, I'm sure it doesn't cover all my sins. Believe me, I want you to walk away from this unscathed as much as you do. This doesn't have to end in violence and bloodshed."

Her face fell into a scowl. "A little late for that, isn't it?"

"It's never too late to stop violence. Believe me, I know."

The three remained in a tense stand-off while Feng quietly moaned and cradled his bloody nose.

The youngest of the three, who had been silent until that moment, finally spoke up. "What happens now?"

The senior agent tossed Nash a pair of handcuffs, which he caught with his right hand. She growled, "We take him in and let the higher-ups sort it out."

Nash thought her course of action wise and well-reasoned. He clicked the cuffs on each wrist and then extended his hands to show they were securely in place. More at ease, both women stepped forward, the youngest holstering her weapon. Both were within arm's length.

That was a mistake.

Nash attacked the senior first; his right jab to her face stunned her enough that he could relinquish her of her weapon. He aimed it at the stunned junior, who stared open-mouthed at the now unsecured handcuffs hanging from his left wrist.

Nash cracked a smile. "Pro tip. Never trust a man who went to magic camp instead of regular camp as a kid."

He leaned down and took her unwisely holstered pistol before patting all three down for additional weapons. Finding none, he took their phones, as well as a shortwave

9

comms device. The last thing he did was take off their boots and tie all the laces together.

"You're... taking our shoes?" the senior woman asked. "Why?"

"It's harder to give chase without shoes. Imagine you somehow get loose? Further imagine you have enough time to catch up with me? I have no wish to harm you, so, if I'm smart, which I like to think I am, I'm going to do everything I can do to slow you down." To emphasise his point, Nash waggled the shoe collection at them.

Handcuffing them all in a nearby temple, he hurried back to the centre of town to arrange immediate transport out. He couldn't afford to go back to his guest house in case it was under surveillance. He would get word to the lovely family to thank them.

As he crossed the bridge, Nash dumped the Chinese weapons, phones and the hiking boots into the river. He had no idea how long he had, but experience told him he had to leave Nepal immediately. His sanctuary had become a cage. He was on the run once more.

If the Chinese could find him in the middle of nowhere, that meant no place on the planet was safe. The time for recovery and reflection was over. It was time to act. He had to contact his team. He had to bring them together. He had to end this once and for all.

CHAPTER

TWO

Every part of Nash's body ached. It had been two weeks since he'd left Kathmandu. Travelling overland from Nepal to Pakistan, he used any conveyance available: local school buses, the back of trucks with a distinct lack of safety features—and functioning brakes—sheep transports and, most painful of all, a busload of singing South African cricket fans. Nash had been through them all and from bunions to scalp, had paid the price. He wasn't twenty anymore. He couldn't sleep through hours upon hours of torturous travel over thousands of kilometres of bumpy, unkept roads.

Compared to the last few weeks, the Islamabad Serena Hotel was out-of-this-world extravagance. He'd tried to convince himself he'd booked into one of the city's most luxurious hotels for the reliable internet connection, but in reality, after weeks of roughing it, he just wanted a very long bath and clean sheets. He'd contemplated utilising the in-house barber, but he needed to fit in with the backpacker set a little longer.

After a ridiculously long sleep on crisp white sheets, he

felt like he could take on the world; which was almost exactly what he was doing.

He fired up his laptop, jumped through several hoops of security and waited for the others to join the video conference. Even with notoriously unsecure hotel wi-fi, Harry had assured him there was no way to trace or eavesdrop on their conversation.

Harry's technical brilliance had enabled her to hack into Tartarus's systems and uncovered some of their deeply buried secrets. Her actions had come at a cost.

Unsurprisingly, his middle-aged rocker of an IT guru was first to jump on. "You look like shit, Nash."

"Love you too, Harry."

The Joan Jett lookalike's demeanour softened. "Missed your stupid face."

"I missed your stupid face, too. How have you been?"

"Fine. And by fine, I mean being in this town is like being trapped with a straightlaced family an hour after Christmas dinner but there's no escape and everyone seems to frown at you if you get drunk and try to have a little fun." She gazed into the distance contemplatively. "Which is *exactly* like my family Christmas dinners."

Having been literally hunted out of her expensive London flat by Tartarus, Harry had been forced into hiding. She was still in Sweden, and evidently still hating it.

Before Nash could reply, a ping indicated another party was connecting. The beaming couple of Eva Destruction and Charles Bishop joined the call, although not as he'd last seen them. Bishop was dressed in beige short-sleeve resort wear and sported a frankly ridiculous bushy moustache. Eva modelled a lightweight shawl over a one-piece bathing suit and was now a blonde.

Harry asked, "Is that an actual backdrop, guys?"

Behind the two former MI6 spies was a lush white sandy beach and a calm incandescent turquoise sea. Eva beamed.

"Yeah, we finally made it to the Maldives. We transited through every airport still using paper processing to get here, avoiding all the big ones. Took us days." She elbowed her companion playfully. "Totally worth it."

Bishop rubbed her arm tenderly before leaning over and kissing her cheek. Nash had never seen them so at peace and loving. It warmed his heart. And it only made this conversation more difficult.

Eva's nose wrinkled. "You're looking suitably rustic, Nash."

"What does that mean?"

"You look like a dirty hippie," Harry answered for her.

"No one travels on in the back of sheep transports for thousands of kilometres in a three-piece suit."

Bishop folded his arms and raised an eyebrow. "Speak for yourself."

Nash chuckled. No matter the circumstance, Bishop was always immaculately dressed. Nash had seen the man descend an elevator shaft dangling from a rope while firing automatic weapons and come out looking like he was ready for the races. He was capital S Style.

There was another ping, and two more faces materialised on-screen. Paul and Nancy Cavendish's background was not as tropical as Eva and Bishop's, nor, it seemed, as warm. The two were rugged up in turtleneck woollen sweaters. Behind them was a misty, grey overcast Scottish morning. Thankfully, Islamabad and the Maldives shared the same time zone, but it was first thing in the morning for Harry, Paul and Nancy in their respective countries.

Paul and Nancy's expressions weren't as sunny as Eva's

and Bishop's, either. It was hardly surprising. Nancy and Paul had been married for years, while Eva and Bishop's relationship had just started. Plus, there was far more for them to be dealing with.

Nash, Eva, Bishop and Paul were all spies. It had been years since Nash had, retired but he still thought himself as a spy. They had all worked under Paul at one point or other. Up until recently, Paul, Eva and Bishop had been happily working for MI6. Then Tartarus came after them.

Although she had never worked in espionage, Harry had been a private detective and had dealt with many undesirables in her time. The woman was as tough as nails. Poor Nancy, on the other hand, had been thrust headfirst into this world without warning, or even a polite request. She'd recently found out not only that her husband worked for MI6, but that Eva, her best friend of many years, was also a spy. And then, because of all their involvements with fighting Tartarus, her husband had been kidnapped before her eyes and she'd been forced into hiding. They'd managed to rescue Paul, but not without cost. Nash could only imagine what the poor woman thought about it all.

"You're all a bunch of fuckers," Nancy stated, folding her arms.

Maybe Nash didn't have to imagine that hard.

There was no hiding Eva's amusement. "It's not like you to verbalise your feelings, Nance. Tell us what you really think."

Her best friend waggled her finger at Eva. "No, you all don't get to be all feckin' smarmy pants. We've all been sent into hiding and if we get caught my feckless husband here informs me it'll likely be treason and we'll be locked away for life. No fair trial, no reasonable discussion, just fuckin' get in the cell and throw away the key. That's *terrifying*. I know you lot are used to this sort of thing and for you it's another bloody Tuesday—"

"It's Friday, my love," Paul pronounced gently.

After a glare that made it clear she didn't care for her husband's correction, Nancy turned to face the screen once more. "But for me this is all brown trouser time. You've bloodied the nose of the biggest and best-funded clandestine bunch of spy cunts the world has ever seen. These bastards have their people in every legit secret service organisation there is. Now every agency believes *we're* the bad guys! They think we've collectively been exploding shit and murdering. They think we're worse than Pol Pot, Hitler, Jeffrey Dahmer and Fred Durst combined. I can't sleep, I can't eat and from what I've heard, you lot have got bugger all way of fixing this. Tell me I'm wrong, I fucken' dare ye." She huffed and before anyone had the chance to respond, she went on. "Love the hair, Eva, by the way, love. You're gorgeous as a raven goddess *and* a blonde bombshell so I have to hate you for that, it's the law."

"I don't think it's as bad as all that," Nash stated.

"Don't you?"

He paused, raised a finger, then dropped it. "Okay, it *is* as bad as all that, but we don't have much of a choice. We fight or we lose. We either take down Tartarus and expose them for the murderous deceptive bastards they are, or we get murdered ourselves or locked up for life. There's no option to sit this one out." Nash leaned forward to emphasise his point. "If the Chinese secret service can find me in the middle of Nepal there's no hiding anywhere. We can sit here and lament our lot in life or we can go on the offensive and take these bastards down once and for all. I for one am ready to destroy their whole castle of lies, even if I have to tear it apart with my own bare hands."

"And you're the pacifist of the group," Harry declared, delight etched across her face. "I may be able to assist. I've been doing some research on the Tartarus board."

Nash had the names memorised: Gabriel Toussaint, Yvon Kerr, Tetsuo Saito, Nathaniel Varco, Hector Kutscher, Nitin Gadkari and his former friend, then enemy and now, who knew what, Jack Pinchot. The members of the board had been confirmed by Pinchot when they'd last spoken, in less than amicable circumstances.

"Research?" Eva asked. "We have the names, but I don't know if there's much we can do in our current circumstances. What do you suggest, we knock on their doors and ask would they like to inform on their organisation, don't mind the treason?"

Harry's brow puckered. "No, I don't think that'll work."

"I was being sarcastic, in case that wasn't obvious," Eva replied in a friendly tone.

"No, I got that." Harry's face turned deadly earnest. "But I wasn't. See, the reason I don't think knocking on the doors of the board members will garner much is because they're all dead."

Harry's statement was met with stunned silence.

"Harry," Bishop gulped, "I think you're going to have expand on that one just a smidge."

The board of Tartarus were the driving force of the organisation. Of the seven members, Pinchot had been the most powerful—until the mysterious head of the organisation had stepped from the shadows and tried to eliminate Pinchot for overstepping his authority. The identity of the head of Tartarus was something Nash was still coming to terms with. He wasn't the only one.

Harry went on. "Almost every one of the Tartarus board has died in the space of forty-eight hours."

"Assassinated?" Eva asked.

"No, of course not." Harry shook her head, her expression dire. "That would be ludicrous. No. They all died of natural causes."

"In the space of a couple of days?" Nash asked.

"Absolutely. Two tragic car crashes on separate continents. One heart attack while at the opera. Three household accidents."

"Accidents?" Nancy asked with the scepticism they all felt.

"I don't know what sort of kinky shit you're into, but in my experience one rarely falls from one's balcony and impales themselves on a fence for fun. Another slipped in the shower, while the last tripped down their stairs."

"Right," Eva exclaimed. "So we're meant to believe that all these people died on the same day coincidentally?"

Harry raised an eyebrow. "What we believe is inconsequential. What the local law enforcement believe is absolutely consequential."

"And they believe there's nothing suspicious here?"

"Apparently. As far as they're concerned these are just one-off, isolated incidents with reasonable explanations." She leaned back. "Of course, we know different."

"It's a purge," Bishop observed.

Paul uncrossed his arms. "They're getting rid of the true believers, those who thought Tartarus was a force for good. Maybe they didn't like the pivot to murder for hire, or maybe they did, and their protests went against the grain once the new leader stepped up." Nash noted Paul hadn't referred to the new leader as his father. "Maybe they don't like whatever the grand scheme is? Who knows?"

Absentmindedly, Eva scratched the back of her head.

"Maybe they should have chosen a better side to begin with?"

Nash frowned. "Wait. Almost every one."

Harry asked, "Come again, Nash?"

"You said almost every one of the Tartarus board have died. You've given us six deaths here. I'm no mathematician, but I believe you're one short. Who's left?"

"I'll give you one guess."

Nash thumped his fist on the desk. "Motherfucker."

"Possibly, you'll have to ask him."

Nancy shook her head in confusion. "What am I missing?"

"Jack Pinchot," Bishop replied, "the one who was leading the board for a while. He's not listed as one of the dead."

Harry spoke again. "Pinchot's the only one of the now former board I can't find. You lot seem to have been the last to see him. That twat is good at disappearing, I'll give him that – they teach them well at the CIA. I can't find a trace of the guy anywhere on the planet and if I'm being modest here, I'm a fucking genius."

"Just because you can't find him doesn't mean he's not dead," Eva suggested. "Tartarus could have found him and eliminated him."

Nash leaned forward. "But they would have made it look like an accident like they did with the others, and made sure it reached the public. The fact there's no trace of him leads me to believe he's still out there somewhere."

"He's the one you let go?" Nancy asked.

"The very same." Paul gave the camera a side eye which Nash suspected was directed at him. "It was believed an embittered ex-Tartarus employee could wreak as much havoc on his former organisation as we could. While we're not allies, we now have a common foe."

"Why did they turn on him?" Nancy asked.

"The…" Paul hesitated awkwardly, "head of Tartarus turned on him when he didn't like the direction Pinchot was taking with the assignation for hire, drug dealing and whatnot. If you believe the brochures, Tartarus was meant to be a beneficial force, with the ability to strike when the established players were hamstrung by bureaucracy and government oversight. He was guiding the ship in the shadows until Pinchot let power go to his head and almost brought them down before they got going. That's when," Paul hesitated again, "the head of Tartarus emerged from the dark and took control."

"That's the second time you've done that," his wife said. "You can say he was your father."

Nancy said what none of the others were brave enough to. Ramsay Cavendish was the former director of MI6, who had retired many years before. Since then, he had recruited senior leaders from various secret service organisations around the world to form the board of Tartarus. He'd then directed them surreptitiously in the background to create the private spy agency without once revealing his identity. The discovery that the head of Tartarus was Paul's estranged father was a fresh and open wound.

On the screen, all eyes turned to Paul. He didn't see them, as he was staring at the ceiling.

"True." He let out a huge sigh before his gaze turned to Nancy. "I can always count on my beautiful wife to get to the crux of any matter." He rubbed her leg tenderly. "It seems with the board eliminated my father is now well and truly in charge. He's our target now. He'd also know perfectly well that will be our aim. He'll be ready for us.

During his tenure at MI6, he garnered a reputation as an unparalleled strategist, a relentless tactician and a ruthless bastard to boot. We underestimate him at our peril."

It was the first time Nash had seen Paul speak openly about his father as the head of Tartarus. The two hadn't spoken for years, mainly due to Paul's terrible upbringing and the fact the men didn't get along as adults either. Nash could only imagine the torment his friend was going through. He also knew Paul well enough to see he was struggling to maintain his impartiality while coming to terms with the fact that his father was now one of the most dangerous men on the planet.

Out of all of them, Paul had the most to deal with. While Ramsay Cavendish had never been a loving father, he was still Paul's flesh and blood. A millstone that was no doubt weighing him down.

"Where's he now?" He turned to his wife, then added with a sad smile, "My father?"

"New York," Harry answered. "He popped up on a few of my alerts yesterday. Not sure where or why, but I'm looking into it. I still have a few backdoor access points into Tartarus, but they removed a lot when they turfed Pinchot. I'm working on it. I'll let you know if I turn anything up."

There was a natural lull in the conversation. So much had been discussed so quickly, they all needed a moment. But Nash felt there was an aspect lacking in their discussion so far. A sense of purpose. He decided to take the lead.

"I see we have a few goals here." He hunkered down in his chair, taking in each of their pixelated faces. "We stop Tartarus and clear our names. So far we've been unsuccessful at both and have gotten nowhere. So, here's what I suggest. We're going to split into two teams. Paul, Nancy, Harry, you're all relatively close, you can be team Alpha."

"I want to know why I'm on a team at all. I'm not a fucken' spy." Nancy frowned, but there was humour in it. "But I'm glad I'm on team Alpha. It sounds kickarse."

Eva crossed her arms. "I want to be Team Alpha."

Nancy poked her tongue out. "Too bad, kiddo, we're already Team Alpha."

"Fine." Eva folded her arms. "We're Team Kickarse then."

"Wait, how come you get to be Kickarse?"

"There's no Team Kickarse," Nash growled.

"Awww, fucknuggets," Eva grumbled.

"Can I be in Team Handsome?" Bishop asked.

"No. And now there's no Team Alpha."

"Hey!" Nancy sat up.

"Paul, Nancy and Harry, you're now Team Ethel and the rest of us are Team Gertrude. That's the end of it." Before there was any more protesting, Nash went on. "Team Ethel, you're the ones with access to technology, so I'm tasking you with finding out what Tartarus's grand scheme is. The way Cavendish referred to it, this is the next phase, what he's been leading up to all along. Whatever it is, it's big. I had the sense it was what was going to give them legitimacy somehow. I want you to find out what the hell they've got planned. You think you can handle that?"

Three nods confirmed they could.

He went on. "Eva, Bishop and I will work on getting inside the head of Tartarus. We need to find out how it operates, who they've recruited in legitimate agencies and most importantly, how to bring it crashing to the ground. There's only one person I know who can do that."

Eva and Bishop's mouths dropped open. Eva was the first to speak.

"Even if we could find him, we're not going to turn

Pinchot." She shook her head. "Correct me if I'm wrong, but in the last conversation you two had, didn't he say the next time he saw you he'd kill you? He's not exactly on our side, dude."

Nash focused on Eva. "I thought you liked a challenge, Eva?"

"I do, but fuck me, there's a difference between a challenge and an impossibility. You may as well ask me to get the Pope, Deepak Chopra and the Dalai Lama in a Gojira mosh pit."

Chuckling, Nash went on. "We *could* turn him, maybe offer protection; they tried to kill him after all. They've murdered the entire board, people he worked closely with for years. He owes Tartarus nothing."

"But equally, he owes you the same, Nash," Bishop observed evenly. "In his eyes, you betrayed him, tortured, kidnapped and deformed him. Sure, you saved his life when you didn't have to, but he's not going to forget the rest of it. He'll always hate you."

Conceding the point with a shrug, Nash replied, "Possibly, but we'll only know if we ask, and before we can, we need to find him. And aren't we lucky that's a Team Gertrude forte?"

In response, both Eva and Bishop rolled their eyes, but with enough good humour that Nash knew he had them onboard.

"We're in the same time zone, so we may as well be in the same room. Got any suggestions where we should rendezvous? We'll need a country close to us. Somewhere way off the beaten track, where no one will ever look."

Eva practically beamed. "I have the place."

If Nash were completely honest, she seemed a little too enthusiastic for his liking.

THREE

The waiter placed the cheese platter in front of Nash, gave a forced smile, then took a few steps back and stood, somewhat awkwardly, by the bar. He must be new, Nash thought—he didn't know the wine list, but he was quick to serve, so it balanced out. Either the young waiter's hairstyle was representative of a rebellious spirit or he'd been attacked by three separate edgy hair stylists, each with their own competing style. Nash couldn't decide which.

Outside the Watsonia Wine Bar it was a quiet chilly overcast Tuesday afternoon. Nash's table looked out to a roundabout adjacent to a suburban train station, neither of which were busy. The wine bar wasn't either. It was certainly pleasant enough with its large windows, exposed brick wall and quaint bar, but Nash couldn't help wondering why he'd spent thirty-six hours of his life travelling here.

He'd caught the first flight out of Islamabad into Singapore. He'd booked a connecting flight to Manila under a false name, but Joel Naoum never made it to the Philippines. As soon as Nash landed he bought a grooming set and clothes and booked himself into an airport lounge to use their private shower facilities. The individual who emerged was, quite literally, a new man. Gone were the raggedy beard, unkempt hair and hippie clothes. In their place was a well-groomed gent sporting a Vandyke beard and a suit. That wasn't all that had changed. Joel become Nathan Farrugia. Nathan boarded a flight to Melbourne, Australia, took a sleeping tablet and was out by the time the plane levelled out.

Nash used every countersurveillance technique he knew to stay ahead of Tartarus. Flipping flights and identities in Singapore would hopefully throw off any trace of his movements—if they'd been picked up at all. He couldn't take chances. It was six of them against the world. Any one of them could be taken down by a simple mistake or worse, put others in danger by not taking every possible precaution. Luckily, Nash was a veteran, so had years of experience to call upon. He chuckled at the thought. It wasn't often he celebrated his advanced years.

Still wondering why he was at the curious little bar, Nash tried an Australian shiraz from the Barossa region. He then spread some French blue cheese on a cracker. Both were exceptional. Maybe the thirty-six hours of travel were worth it. He straightened his back and a jolt of pain shot up his left side. Maybe not.

After his second shiraz, Nash's back felt better. By the third he'd completely forgotten about it. About to order a fourth, he heard a cry from the doorway.

"Oi! Who let this pommy git in?"

Smiling without turning around, he simply hoisted his middle finger proudly in the air. In seconds he was engulfed in a bear hug. Eva and Bishop squeezed him tight. He turned and hugged them properly. It was more like greeting old friends than it was colleagues fighting for their very lives. As they sat, Nash concluded that perhaps they *were* friends. Nothing forged a unique bond quite like shared hardship. Eva and Bishop weren't associates, they were true and genuine friends, the kind who came along rarely and stayed with you for the rest of your life. However long that may be.

Nash was still getting used to Eva's blonde locks. Uncharacteristically wearing a dress, which showed off her countless tattoos, she came across as elegant but with an edge. Bishop, as always, was dressed immaculately in a three-piece suit. Even in suburban Melbourne, he couldn't be anything but debonair, despite the best efforts of his ridiculous moustache.

They sat at a table, and Nash was able to focus on their faces. "What the hell happened to you two?" he asked.

It had only been a few days since Nash had seen them on video conference, but since then Eva had somehow gained a black eye and Bishop sported a plaster over a purple contusion on his temple.

"Uh, that's going to have to wait until after a wine." Eva waved to the waiter. "Lots of wine."

The waiter arrived with a pad and pencil. "Sorry, we don't have any music—the wi-fi is out."

"I know."

Three heads swivelled to Bishop. He waved an apologetic hand and said, "I'll have a glass of the chianti. Eva?"

Glancing at the menu, she replied, "The Yarra Valley pinot noir, please. And a bowl of the olives with garlic and rosemary."

The waiter's forehead creased into confusion. He

seemed to be writing in longhand. "Yarrat something pinot grigio... and what was the first one?"

"Yarra Valley pinot *noir*," Eva corrected him. "And the chianti."

"C-h-i-a-n-t-i ," he said while writing. "Got it. Thanks."

They exchanged glances as if to say, *he's new*, then moved on quickly.

Once the waiter was out of earshot Nash asked Bishop in a low voice, "You knew the wi-fi is out? You just arrived."

"I may have had something to do with it." Bishop shot finger guns at a security camera in a corner above the bar. "I took their internet out a few hours ago, in case they're connected to the cloud. I don't want our faces showing up and activating an alert of some sort. I can do without Michael Bublé for an evening if it means I don't get shot in the face."

Eva inclined her head as if to say, *fair*. "Personally, I've always said I'd prefer to get shot in the face than listen to Michael Bublé." She poked Nash and motioned to the room. "What do you think?"

"Of the bar, the city or the country?"

Eva leaned forward. "Yes."

Nash hesitated. He knew Eva was proud of her country of birth. Her obsession with coffee came from the city's infamous snobbery on the subject.

"I get it when you say this city is coffee obsessed. I tried to order a cappuccino at Melbourne airport and the moustachioed barista stared me dead in the eye and said, 'no'. He didn't say anything else, just stared me down until I ordered a flat white."

"No, you didn't!" Eva was gobsmacked. "You tried to order a cappuccino *in Melbourne*?"

Nash help up a defensive palm. "I wanted one, okay? I

didn't know it was a criminal offence here. I'd just fought off three Chinese secret service operatives and there I was, intimidated by a haughty hipster—and he *won*. If that's not proof of how seriously this city takes its coffee then I don't know what is."

"I haven't been home in years, but as soon as I stepped off the plane it was like someone enveloped me in a warm blanket. This city gives me the warm fuzzies. I forgot how much I loved it. Sure, it's not as obvious as Sydney or London and doesn't have the big touristy attractions, but there's a whole subculture of laneway bars where there are no signs or even shopfronts. The coolest bars are in piss-smelling laneways behind unmarked doors. It's like the city deliberately makes you dig deeper and you're rewarded all the more for it."

Nash motioned to the bar they were in. "Then why meet out here in suburbia?"

Eva turned coy. "Partly because I've been to this bar before, partly because it's way off the beaten track, but mainly because I thought it was funny. I mean, it would probably be voted the least likely location for a meeting planning world shaping events... if anyone even knew where it was."

"I did wonder." Nash chuckled. "Are you staying with family while you're here?"

Eva gave him a sad smile. "None left, I'm afraid. My folks died quite a while back."

"I'm sorry."

Eva waved a hand, dismissing the comment. "I came to terms with it long ago. No relatives left here or anywhere else. Apparently, I had a great aunt who went off to Hollywood in the seventies or eighties or thereabouts and made a few scream queen movies. She was big for about ten minutes, then became a detective or something. Mum never talked about her when I was growing up, but older relatives called her the black sheep of the family." Her eyes danced with humour. "Well, until I turned up anyway. She'd be my only living relative if she's still around." She moved a coaster around the table. "I won't be looking up friends on this trip. Can't put them in danger, not after what we've been through." Eva stopped and became more serious. "Did you see Harry's latest?"

"We're really not going to talk about your injuries?" Nash asked.

"Wine," Eva said with a humorous tone, but Nash detected an undercurrent of something he couldn't quite put his finger on. "We're waiting for the wine."

"Fine," Nash replied. "I haven't been able to check my messages," he turned to Bishop, "wi-fi is out. What did I miss?"

Uncharacteristically, neither Eva nor Bishop answered immediately. In fact, Nash detected a certain level of dread in their features. An unusual state for them both.

Leaning in, Nash asked, "What's going on?"

Fidgeting, Eva rubbed her palms on her jeans. "Just when we thought Tartarus couldn't get more douchebaggerly they go and out douchebag themselves by, like, a factor of a million douchebags."

She was stalling, Nash wasn't entirely sure why. Eva was the one who'd brought it up. "What aren't you telling me?"

The two exchanged glances and leaned in conspiratorially. Bishop spoke in a hushed tone.

"We have a lead, of sorts. Harry dug around Tartarus's servers, the ones she hacked into with Pinchot's credentials, and created background admin accounts before

Pinchot's access was removed. She used them last night and uncovered what she's sure is a lead on the so-called grand scheme."

Nash let out a whistle. The grand scheme was what former MI6 Director Ramsay Cavendish—Paul's father— had referred to mid-gloat, believing Nash was about to die. It had been clear he fervently believed this grand scheme would bring back old-school statecraft and manipulate governments on a scale that hadn't occurred since the Cold War. He was adamant he'd found a way to bring back old-fashioned espionage to manipulate the world as he saw fit. Nash still felt a chill of fear thinking about it. It wasn't necessarily the words Cavendish had sprouted, more the unwavering fervour in his eyes. He was a zealot. Worse, he was a zealot with means.

"What did Harry find out?"

"There's a file, I shit you not, called 'Ultimate Sacrifice'."

Nash gave a groan. "Cavendish isn't fucking around, is he? Subtle is not in this man's vocabulary."

Bishop went on. "The subtly named 'Ultimate Sacrifice' mentions finding a terrorist cell and fooling them into believing they're doing their organisation's good work and giving the bad guys the means to carry it out. Everything would be completely real. Bombs, terrorists, taking inno-cent lives. Tartarus would warn the legitimate spy agencies ahead of time. If they believed Tartarus, they'd hand over all their supposed intel and take all the credit."

"And if not?" Nash suspected the answer but dreaded hearing it.

Eva placed her hands on her knees. "Tartarus will let the terrorists explode a massive bomb, killing potentially thousands, all in the name of legitimising Tartarus on the world stage. They'll spin it that Tartarus could have prevented the carnage if only the old inept and decrepit agencies had listened. The ultimate I fucken' told you so. They'll milk it, and manipulate public opinion in their favour." Her shoulders slumped despondently. "Harry's going to contact us if she discovers more."

Nash leaned back. "Jesus Christ."

The couple remained silent, not about to argue. Bishop spoke first.

"Harry's evidence is vague but significant. It kind of fits with what Cavendish was describing, doesn't it? Creating an event to afford them legitimacy. Thwarting a terrorist plot and saving the day fits his goals."

"Did you just use 'thwarting' in a sentence?" Eva raised an eyebrow. "You've changed."

They halted their conversation as the waiter arrived and dispensed their drinks and nibbles with a heavy hand. The glasses were filled generously. Nash assumed it must be the Australian way, they even served wine boisterously.

His head spun. He knew Cavendish was evil, but murdering thousands to unironically be perceived as the good guys? The man was truly twisted. Nash would review all Harry had and try to make sense of it. Bishop was right, it fit exactly what Cavendish had outlined as his grand scheme. It was a chilling turn of events.

Nash motioned to the faces opposite him. "Speaking of uncovering truths, you have your wine, now tell me how the hell you sustained these injuries?"

Eva took a gulp of wine. "As a bit of an indulgence we'd booked one of those over the water cabins at this luxury resort. The ones where you can literally roll out of bed and into the ocean. It was glorious. Well, it was, until it wasn't. We were, uh, enjoying our last night in the Maldives when it happened."

Bishop playfully elbowed her. "I was certainly enjoying myself."

Giving her man a wrinkle of her nose, she turned to Nash. "We were having sex."

Nash crinkled his forehead. "Is this really relevant to the story?"

In unison, they both answered, "Yes."

Eva went on. "We were having a lovely old time when from my vantage point I saw a shadow pass by the window."

"I'm probably going to regret asking this," Nash winced, "but 'vantage point'?"

Eva thrust one horizontal palm in the air. "Bishop." The other she placed above it, vertically. "Me. Got it?"

"Unfortunately, yes."

Eva went on. "We were at the far end of the resort, there was no reason for anyone to be there that late at night. So I paused activities while we grabbed our pistols from under our pillows."

"You both keep guns under your pillows?"

Bishop took a sip of wine. "Doesn't everyone?"

Ignoring him, Eva continued her tale. "Three seconds later two men burst in, guns blazing. Luckily they had no idea where in the room we were, so their bullets were indiscriminate." Her face was uncharacteristically serious. "Ours weren't. We took them out with minimal fuss."

"Efficient work. But it doesn't explain the..." Nash motioned around his face.

"Getting to that. Once we'd dressed, packed and searched the bodies we discovered two more goons at the end of the pier. They put up more of a fight. Once we eliminated them we bugged out as soon as we could. We bribed airport staff to keep us hidden and they let us board at the last possible second. We haven't slept since."

She waved her empty glass at the waiter, gesturing for another. Bishop did the same; Nash was still nursing his drink.

"Did you learn anything?" Nash asked.

"Yes," Bishop said earnestly.

"What's that?"

"Eva clenches when she fires. Every time she pulled the trigger, she... grasps, you know?" He grinned roguishly. "I like it."

Eva tutted. "I'm not going to make a habit of firing weaponry when we have sex, Bishop."

He frowned. "Let's leave it as an option is all I'm asking."

"You're incorrigible."

"But you love me."

She gave him a humorous side eye. "Against my better judgement."

Nash rolled his eyes. "I meant, did you find anything about those who attacked you?"

Both shook their heads. Bishop spoke first.

"Whoever they were, they were professional. No clothing labels, guns stripped of serial numbers, no IDs, credit cards, nothing. They were well trained." He popped an olive in his mouth. "But we were better. My guess is Tartarus, but it's just that, a guess. They were Caucasian, but we didn't have any fireside chats to identify accents, so we don't know. And we didn't hang around to ask many questions."

Nash nodded, accepting the logic of their strategy, but also in contemplation. First the attack on him in Nepal, then on Bishop and Eva in the Maldives. In both instances they'd thought they were safe, untraceable. In both instances they'd been so very wrong. The walls were closing in.

It was becoming clear that despite their best efforts, nowhere in the world was safe. They'd left their previously used fake passports in train stations in seedy locations around the world. Inevitably some punk would try and use them, or get caught selling them, be identified and create a false flag, prompting multiple law enforcement agencies to converge on a confused criminal with a fake ID and a stunned expression.

But despite all this, they were still getting found in even the most remote parts of the planet. Nash put his glass down conclusively, with such force that Eva and Bishop jumped.

"Enough of this bullshit." Nash clenched and unclenched his fists. "We need to find Pinchot and turn him. This sitting around and waiting to get picked off is getting tedious. It's time we take this fight to Tartarus. Let's strategize our options."

Over the next hour, that's exactly what they did. The three drew up a list of names, people they'd worked with at MI6 and CIA who would be likely targets for recruitment. They'd supply the names to Harry and have her perform a forensic accountant investigation, looking for any sign of the hand of Tartarus. Then they'd strike.

Next, they turned their attention to finding Pinchot. That was the harder of their two tasks. Pinchot was a master of the espionage craft. If he didn't want to be found, it would be next to impossible to do so. Then again, until recently, Nash thought he was equally good at concealing his existence, and that had proven to be a misplaced belief.

No one could remain hidden forever. At least, that was the hope.

Bishop gently used his thumb to remove a tiny piece of rosemary from Eva's lip. His hand lingered on her face. It was a tender and subtle gesture. In return, she nuzzled into his palm and pulled him in for a kiss.

Looking in Nash's direction, Eva asked, "Everything alright? You looked okay, then suddenly sad."

"Fine." Nash stared down at the table. "That's the knee jerk reply, isn't it? *Fine.* It's more, seeing you two so in love and happy despite *everything* reminded me of what I don't have. Even before this whole Tartarus mess I was happy enough, content enough. It was my choice to remain single, to be unburdened... wow, that's too harsh a word, isn't it? What's a better one? To be *unbound* by an ongoing relationship. For a long time that was for compassionate reasons; I was hardly in a profession where I could guarantee I'd be home every night for dinner. After I retired, I don't know, maybe I thought I was too old, maybe I was still in the habit of pushing long-term relationships away, I don't know." Nash swirled his drink. "Sorry, got a bit maudlin."

Bishop said, "That's a longwinded way of saying you're lonely."

Nash tapped the table twice and pointed to him in agreeance.

Eva wrinkled her nose. "Did you ever want to get married, have kids and all that?"

"There were fleeting moments. Neither ever happened. I had two women propose to me, but they fizzled out. As for the kid thing, it never would have worked with my lifestyle." He twirled the stem of his wine glass. "Life would have been different, for sure. Too late now for that sort of thing anyway."

"Did you ever think of contacting past girlfriends?" Eva asked. "The ones you almost married? Who was the French spy who stole your heart, Sophia? Ever think of giving her a call?"

"Nearly every day."

"And?"

"I never have."

"You're not dead yet."

"Not for lack of trying on Tartarus's behalf," Nash replied with a close approximation of a smile. "But, ah, Sophia wouldn't answer, I'm sure. Reasonably sure. Somewhat sure? Things didn't end badly, but it definitely ended when it should have."

"So..." Eva traced her finger around the tabletop. "Finding Pinchot is super important, right?"

"Oh, we're back talking tactics are we?" Bishop asked, waving at the waiter for more wine.

"This is kind of tangentially aligned, Bishop," she replied. "Pinchot, to the best of our knowledge, never left France."

"We don't know that," Bishop replied. "We just don't have proof that he has. Those are two completely disparate things."

"Granted," Eva went on. "If we assume Pinchot never left France, or at the very least require evidence that he did, and there may be a clue as to his next destination..."

Nash could see Eva was leading somewhere but wished she'd get to the point.

"... then logic would dictate we could possibly ask the Frenchies if they have anything at all on Pinchot."

"Ask?" Bishop frowned. "One doesn't ask an intelligence agency... oh..."

Eva's lips pursed mischievously. "Hey Nash, you know anyone in French intelligence who you can trust?"

"Oh, hell no." Nash shook his head violently. "No no no no no. No way. No chance in hell." He folded his arms. "Nope."

Fluttering her eyelids, Eva asked, "Is that a yes?"

Groaning, Nash asked, "Is this to find Pinchot or set me up on a date?"

Eva raised her palms. "Why not both?" Her tone turned serious. "You said Sophia still works for Direction générale de la Sécurité extérieure. You also told us she was bloody good at what she did and that you trust her unquestioningly. Well, trusted, past tense. My point is, if you have an in at the DGSE who you're reasonably certain hasn't been turned by Tartarus then you should absolutely talk to her."

"And," Bishop added, "if it happens to be over a candlelit dinner, so be it."

While Nash could see their point, he didn't necessarily want to. The thought of seeing Sophia again filled him with both excitement and dread. They had been spectacular together, for a time. She was the love of his life and he should have fought harder to keep her, but in the end their conflicting schedules, separate countries and career ambitions had defeated them in a way no foe ever could.

He still dreamed of her. In his more sombre moments, he still longed for her. Eva had asked why he hadn't contacted Sophia after he'd retired: the truth was he'd been too scared to. Scared she'd moved on. Scared she hadn't but still wouldn't want to see him. Scared she did want to see him, but they couldn't rekindle the love they'd once shared. Scared they could.

If the fight against Tartarus had taught him anything it was that he shouldn't sit life out in the safe confines of the shadow of doubt. His life wasn't over. It was time he forged a new one full of happiness and left regret behind. He should have contacted Sophia. He should have done a great many things. Now, with everything closing in around him, he feared his time was almost up.

While Eva and Bishop's logic was sound, in the end he settled for the safest response.

"I'll think about it."

As the waiter brought another round, Nash's attention was drawn to the street outside. Two men milled about on the far side of the roundabout. In itself, that was nothing unusual, except they were huddled close enough to suggest they knew each other but hadn't exchanged a word in the last twenty minutes. The more Nash observed, the more he saw they were purposefully not looking at the bar. They were watching everything *but* the bar. The moment the grey-haired man spoke into his sleeve, Nash's instincts kicked in.

Raising his glass, Nash spoke in a low voice. "I can't be sure, but I think we've been made. Two suspects diagonally across the other side of the roundabout. Suspicious stakeout vibes. The one on the left just spoke into his cuff. At least pretend to use a mobile phone, man. Come on, that's sloppy."

Eva and Nash were experienced enough not to gaze in the direction Nash indicated, not immediately anyway. They took their time, acting as naturally as they could while casting a casual glance towards the two men.

"Sketchy as fuck." Eva leaned in for some olives. "How we playing this?"

"If they're using comms devices they're not alone." Bishop eyed the waiter, making sure he was out of earshot. "We could be surrounded. There's no back door to this place, so I suggest we pay up and casually make our way to the train station and see if we're followed. Once mobile we can re-strategize from there. Plan?"

"Plan," Nash and Eva concurred.

Standing, Nash realised he was more intoxicated than he'd thought. Not drunk, but not entirely sober either. *Damn this getting old shit.* Gone were the days of downing a bottle of wine before going drinking. He pushed through it, unsure whether *it* was the fuzzy semi-drunk feeling or his lamentations at getting older.

He was reminded of his friend Sebastian Hawk. They'd formed a bond when they were in the SAS, and as the principal of the local school at Devil's End, Hawk had given Nash his teaching job. A few years older than Nash, Hawk once claimed he drank less as he grew older and simply stood up quickly for the same effect. Nash didn't necessarily believe it—he'd seen the man down a bottle of Jack Daniels and go on to chair a flawless parent-teacher evening.

Eva paid their bill, thanked the underworked waiter and the three made their way to the exit.

"No tip?" Nash asked.

Eva shook her head. "This is Australia, mate. Hospitality staff get paid a good wage with all the benefits, so unless someone actively sucks your dick during the night, Aussies don't generally leave a tip."

"Uh, fair enough, I guess."

Bishop brought Eva up to speed. "When you paid, the two outside moved off, one talking into his sleeve again. We've certainly got company. Nash, you armed?"

"Negative. I pretty much came directly here from the airport. You?"

Bishop shook his head. "Like tipping, this country looks

down on guns. Ownership is severely limited, so we haven't been able to source any." Bishop cracked his neck. "This could be interesting."

Nash flexed and unflexed his hands. "What are we thinking? Tartarus? ASIO? MI6? CIA?"

Bishop inhaled deeply. "My money's on SHISH."

"SHISH?" A crease formed between Eva's brows. "Who the hell is SHISH?"

"Albania's State Intelligence Service. I hardly ever get to bring up SHISH. It's honestly the best intelligence agency name. Say it with me: SHISH."

Ignoring the request, Nash grimaced. "I feel like you two aren't taking this as seriously as you should."

"I assure you, they're not SHISH, the CIA or any of those."

All three turned to see the waiter. And his gun. Mainly the gun.

The waiter held a Beretta at waist height, pointed at the three of them. His expression was grim, his grip firm. They were unarmed and he had the drop on them.

Nash turned ever so slightly towards Eva. "You really should have tipped him."

FOUR

Bishop folded his arms. "I thought you said weapons were hard to come by in this country, and yet here's this humble waiter waving one about like it's nothing at all."

"I'm not a humble waiter," the not-humble-waiter replied.

That explained the generous pours and the confused order taking. It was hard to detect an accent. When he was a heavy-handed waiter he'd sounded Australian enough, but now less so; regionless in a practiced way.

"To get the drop on the three of us, no, you're not," Bishop conceded. He let out a bored moan. "Whose turn is it?"

Blinking several times, the man asked, "Turn for what?"

"I did the last one," Eva replied.

"Uh," Bishop raised a finger, "no, you didn't. That was me."

"What are you lot on about?" The gunman's face was a mass of confusion.

Eva shook her head. "I did the guy. You know, the guy

40

with the thing." She waved her hand to her side. "The arm thing."

Bishop's well-manicured features broke into a scowl. "That wasn't the last one."

"It totally was."

"Do you not," the man's confusion hadn't dissipated one iota, "see the gun? What are you talking about?"

Bishop waved an index finger in the air. "I think it's you, Nash. We can't seem to decide ourselves."

Shaking his head, Nash replied, "Pacificism, remember?"

His protestations notwithstanding, Nash realised the others weren't positioned correctly.

Raising an index finger on his free hand, the not-humble-waiter interjected, "Whatever you lot are on about, I wa—"

Nash struck like a cobra. One instant the gun was in the man's hand, the next it was in Nash's. Before the shock had fully formed on his face, Nash followed through with a bone-crunching elbow to the side of his head. It was more of a reflex than a conscious decision.

As the man hit the floor, out cold, Nash offered a weak, "Sorry."

Hefting an eyebrow, Bishop eyed the gun in Nash's hand. "This pacifism thing of yours seems quite fluid, I must say."

"It's a matter of degrees."

The comment amused Bishop. "How so?"

Motioning to the prone man, Nash replied, "There was a time I would have just snapped his neck."

"And yet, I'm not sure he's going to wake up and thank you."

"The fact he can thank me or not is proof of my evolution. All I can do is be the best I can in the present moment. That's all any of us can hope to do. The real test of nonviolence lies in being brought into contact with those who have contempt for it. Mahatma Gandhi said that."

Eva looked out the window. "What do you think?"

"I think anyone who quotes Gandhi is smarter than I am." Bishop smirked.

Groaning good-naturedly, Eva replied, "I meant about our friends outside." Her eyes scanned the grey streets. "It would have been good to keep him conscious. How are we going to ask him questions now?"

"With his friends outside somewhere, I doubt we'd have had much of an opportunity." Nash slipped the Beretta into the back of his jeans under his jacket.

"The man makes a good point," Bishop conceded.

All three had their game faces on. Whoever was after them, they were armed, well manned and proficient in the ways of espionage. How else could they have traced them to the remote bar even before they'd arrived? They were no slouches, therefore they had to be treated as worthy adversaries, and—Nash felt the weight of the Beretta—likely deadly ones.

Eva took a hair tie from her pocket and tied her hair into a ponytail, a move Nash recognised as showing she meant business. Bishop picked up two cheese knives from a nearby tray. Nash's hand rested on the pistol under his jacket. They opened the glass door.

Even with the grey clouds, there were still a smattering of people on the streets. Frequent cars entered the roundabout. A train could be heard as it forged its way through the rail trench nearby.

The three turned left towards the station. They made it all of five steps. On each side of the road stood two pairs of thick-set men. All wore similar long black coats. All sported an intensity and stared directly at the three of them.

"Maybe we should..." Eva thumbed in the other direction.

"Good call."

The three quietly headed away from the black-coats, across the bridge over the rail trench. They didn't make it far before they saw another set of four black-coats coming the other way. They couldn't go forward. They couldn't go back. They were trapped, with the black-coats closing in.

"I have a proposal." Nash eyed the nearby station. A train's horn sounded as passengers disembarked. "And I don't think either of you are going to like it."

Eva was the first to cotton on. Her face instantly changed. Nash wasn't sure if she liked the idea or not.

"Oh, get fucked." She shook her head. "Get royally fucked with a corgi."

Nash was reasonably certain she didn't like the idea.

"What..." Bishop started before his face morphed as well. "You can't be serious? See those things? They're electrical wires. And the train? They move!"

Nash heard another horn, indicating the train was about to depart. They didn't have long.

"It's just about to leave the station, it's not at full speed." The words sounded uncertain, even to his own ears.

"And when it is at full speed?" Eva asked.

"Hold on and hope for the best." Nash grimaced. "That's always been my philosophy in life."

The black-coats walked faster, as if sensing what was about to transpire. Nash was the first to move. Rushing to the railing, he hoisted one leg over, followed by the other. There was a small ridge at the base of the overpass and he held both hands on the railing, leaning into the void. Eva and Bishop reluctantly followed suit, bunching together about the width of a train carriage.

The train left the station.

The black-coats broke into a run.

Nash, Eva and Bishop crouched in readiness.

The blue and silver train gathered speed.

One of the female black-coats yelled, "Don't!"

The three leapt off the overpass.

The landing was worse than Nash anticipated; and he'd anticipated it would be bad.

Landing with a thud, Nash lost his footing immediately on top of the moving six-carriage train. Thankfully he sprawled forward instead of sideways, so when he face planted with an "oof" it was on top of the train rather than next to it, or worse, under it. Eva was right behind him and her landing was slightly more elegant, but still she toppled forward and landed on all fours. Bishop, on the other hand, landed with aplomb, remained standing and somehow managed to be debonair at the same time. He tugged his cuffs and raised a smug eyebrow. *How does he do that?*

Bishop frowned at Nash, impressed. "Not bad for an octogenarian."

"Don't make me chase you with my walking frame," Nash yelled to be heard over the increasing wind. "Also, fuck you."

Eva tutted. "Such spice from grandpa."

The train sped through pleasant-looking neighbourhoods on one side and native parklands on the other. The three had to yell to be heard.

"Who the hell where they?" Eva asked.

"I think the most immediate question is, can they follow us? Maybe they can catch up with the train?"

Eva gave Nash an amused shake of her head. "I think

you're seriously overestimating the efficiency of the Melbourne road system." She hunkered down as the train made a slight turn. "We could get off at the next station, or the one after, but they're likely thinking the same. The more stations we pass, the more chances they have of losing us. Let's ride this all the way into the city, where it will be easier to disappear."

"Might I suggest," Bishop interrupted, raising a finger, "we ride the remainder of the journey via the interior of this public transport conveyance? It's playing havoc with my hair."

Eva's dress flapped up and she was forced to push it down. "Yeah, let's worry about your hair, shall we?"

In deference to Bishop's coiffure concerns, the three hunkered down until the next station. As the train rolled into Macleod Station, the three slid down the side of the carriage and entered through the automatic doors unnoticed. They sat on the multicoloured seats facing one another, eyeing fellow passengers for any sign of threat, but the smattering of commuters were more concerned with their mobile devices than the windswept new arrivals. The doors closed, and as the train left the station the team leaned in close.

"Any idea who our new friends are?" Bishop asked.

"Apart from getting a bulk deal on black coats, no clue." Nash rubbed his stubble. "But I don't intend to hang around long enough to find out, either. Sorry Eva, but I'm afraid a tour of your old stomping ground would be unwise at this juncture."

"Damn it." Eva crossed her arms. "I was going to drag you guys along to Degraves, Gertrude Street, Queen Vic, Mrs Parmas, the Tote, Cherry, *all* the laneway bars," her hands flew outward, "everywhere."

"I assume all those words mean something?" Nash asked.

Eva growled. "Shame it's all off the cards. I'd love to give you guys the works. You wouldn't sleep for days."

"Perhaps next time, my love?" Bishop patted her knee. "Preferably when people aren't trying to kill us."

The train travelled up an incline and Nash looked out the window to see a raised train station, above a nearby road. The stop at Rosanna Station came and went without any black-coated individuals boarding the train. Despite himself, Nash began to relax. Whoever it was would have a hard time catching them now.

His mind turned to how their foes had found them. Who were they? Where did they fit into the whole scheme of things? In fact, what *was* the whole scheme of things? If Harry's investigations were anything to go by, they now had a planned terrorist attack to contend with as well as taking down Tartarus and evading every major spy agency on Earth. It was a lot.

Were Tartarus truly evil enough to orchestrate a terrorist attack all in the name of acceptance? Were they that morally bereft as to believe taking thousands of innocent lives was a fair price for their entry onto the world stage? It was a horrifying thought. If Cavendish believed this was a valid course of action, where would he draw the line? Would there ever be a line? Nash suspected he knew the answer.

Doing his best to shake off the encroaching malaise, Nash glanced absentmindedly about the carriage. "This seems safe." Realising he needed to elaborate, he went on. "Public transport, I mean. The passengers seem relaxed and everything is clean. It fits, I guess. All the Australians I've met seem agreeable most of the time."

Eva's index finger sliced the air. "Don't you believe it, mate. Ask two Aussies if Vegemite goes in the fridge or the cupboard, or if it's called a potato cake or a potato scallop, or about the date for Australia Day and you'll soon find out we're not so agreeable."

"Fine," Nash chuckled. "But what I'm saying is you never had a civil war."

"I don't know, if you bring up the potato cake thing I reckon you'll come pretty close."

For the remainder of the twenty-minute journey the three continued their conversation, mainly focused on the threat of the terrorist attack. While the thought was abhorrent, academically, Nash could see the thinking behind it. Nothing instilled fear in the general populace like the threat of a random attack on home soil. Wars were horrible, yes, but for a large portion of the population war was theoretical, abstract. Terrorism was very real and fear inducing—which was exactly the point. Tartarus becoming the hero of such a catastrophic and notorious event would cement their validity in the minds of the espionage community and the wider world. Cavendish would get what he'd been after all along: legitimacy. Once that happened it would be next to impossible to bring the juggernaut down. Their little band of misfits couldn't compete with that. Tartarus would have won. With nothing further to add to the topic, the three stared out the windows for a while, the passing scenery doing nothing to lift their spirits.

Nash moved on to the next pressing topic: strategizing about how and when they'd leave the country. The most obvious move would be to get to the airport as soon as possible. But whoever their attackers were, the airport would be the most logical place to search. Instead, the course of action they settled on was to buy an old car, drive it to South Australia and fly out from there. It would add days to their plan but was by far the safest option, and given recent encounters, safer was preferred.

As the train neared the city centre, Nash was afforded a better view of the skyline. It was pretty, a mixture of unique modern skyscrapers and classic architecture. Melbourne was a clean city, apart from the requisite graffiti adorning every flat surface facing the rail line, the same the world over. They passed the famous MCG, and Nash tried to remember the last time he'd seen a cricket match. The train slowed and entered a tunnel as the automated announcement informed them they were heading into Flinders Street Station. Eva stood; Bishop and Nash followed suit. They'd reached their stop.

They alighted the train and headed up an escalator. Nash saw daylight through grand leadlight windows above clocks with different train line names underneath. Outside, cars honked and trams dinged as they passed through the busy intersection. The station was far older than the other more modern stations they'd passed through. This was more an Edwardian Baroque design. Melbourne was a hodgepodge of different styles mangled together to make something unique, Nash concluded. It seemed fitting that this was Eva's city.

Walking in front of Nash and Bishop, Eva stopped dead, causing the two men to barrel into her.

"Ah, balls." She screwed her face to one side. "I forgot about this. We have to go through barriers, and without a valid pass we can't get out."

Dozens of commuters flooded through the automated barriers, tapping cards to open yellow gates. Uniformed officers watched with eagle eyes as nearby police officers milled about casually.

"We could say we lost our tickets," Bishop suggested.

"All three of us at the same time?" Eva asked sceptically. "How good are you guys at hurdles?"

"Terrible," Nash replied, stony-faced. "I presently have the flexibility of the Tin Man after he's been left out in the rain." Nash motioned for the others to follow him. "Never mind, I've got this." He approached the friendliest looking uniformed rail officer, a woman in her mid-thirties. He gave her his best toothy grin. "Excuse me," Nash said in his thickest English accent, "my friends and I seem to have made a grave mistake. We're new to your lovely city and boarded a train at Jolimont," Nash recalled the station because of its silly name, "expecting to purchase a ticket from an inspector, but it seems we were misinformed, as there were none. It appears we should have purchased a card of some description beforehand. Could you assist us, please?"

The woman smiled, lighting up her face. "That's only one stop. Tell you what..." Her bright green eyes swivelled from side to side. "... as long as you buy a myki card before you next get on public transport, I don't think you're going to send the state of Victoria broke." She pressed a button and the gate before her opened. She gave him a wink. "Enjoy your stay."

Eva and Bishop went through hand in hand, waving their thanks. As Nash passed, the inspector leaned forward and in a smoky voice added, "I get off in an hour."

Not sure how to respond, Nash gave her a stunned wave and walked through the barriers. Outside, Melbournians of all descriptions darted in countless directions on the wide streets. Lines snaked out from takeaway stalls beneath the awnings of the station's exterior.

Striding towards the main intersection, Eva slapped

Nash's arm. She made an *oh* shape with her lips. "Duuuu-ude! You totally grey-foxed that chick!"

"Shut up."

"We've been going about this all wrong! Why are we even fighting anyone when you could just seduce them and be done with it?"

Nash replied, "Did I mention shut up?"

Eva danced from one foot to the other. "Hell, maybe Cavendish will let this all slide if you just put out?"

Nash groaned. "I'm glad you find this so amusing."

Bishop looked on, equally amused, right up until the second he wasn't. In an instant his face grew gravely serious.

"Black-coats, nine o'clock."

Without looking around, Eva responded in a low voice, "What the cinnamon toasted fuck did you just say?"

"Two," Bishop grunted. "No, make that four black-coats converging on our position. We've been made."

"How did they get here so quickly?"

"Let's worry about that later." Bishop thumbed behind them. "I suggest we make our way across the bridge to the other side of the Yarra."

"What's a Yarra?" Nash asked.

"The river."

The three did an about-face and strode purposefully through the throng of pedestrians, away from the four black-coats. It had recently rained, and the coats blended in with the rest of the city's inhabitants. In fact, nearly everyone was wearing black. Perhaps that was the Melbournian dress code, Nash thought. There was no time to ask. They reached the long bridge and walked across it as briskly as they could without raising suspicion.

The old Princes Bridge afforded a wonderful view of the

city, showing off a fancy building with a tall spire. Restaurants and bars overlooked the waterway, and a few bars even floated on the river itself. Various boats casually meandered down the Yarra. The city looked sophisticated and inviting. It was a pity Nash had no time to enjoy the view. The three powered on.

"Why's the water brown?" Bishop asked as they practically jogged along the footpath.

"It's always like that," Eva growled. "It's an upside-down river."

Reaching the other side of the bridge, the three raced down a set of steps. Behind him, Nash caught a glimpse of two of the black-coats glaring directly at him. He took the steps three at a time.

The paved walkway hosted restaurants on one side and the river on the other. An occasional tourist boat was moored with steps down to the vessels. Eva, Nash and Bishop broke into a run.

They didn't get far.

In the distance, two more black-coats advanced towards them. Nash recognised one of them as the grey-haired man who'd been stationed opposite the wine bar.

They skidded to a halt and turned to see the four black-coats slow and advance. They were hemmed in.

Head pivoting from side to side, Eva grunted. "Haemorrhoids on a pogo stick. They've got us cornered."

Bishop looked towards the river. "Are they barbecues? On a boat?"

He was right. Four small metal dinghies powered by outboard motors were tied to a little jetty. The seats around the edge of each boat faced a hotplate at its centre. Eva descended the stairs, followed by the others. She leaned down and began to untie a mooring line.

"You're going to steal a boat?" Bishop asked incredulously.

Eva continued working on the rope, undaunted. "It's either that or swim."

Bishop leaned down and helped her. "Floating bars, upside down rivers, boats with barbecues. What sort of city is this?"

Before the line was untied the black coats blocked the top of the stairs and descended, each with one hand menacingly in their coat pocket. They'd run out of time. Shadows enveloped their huddled forms. Nash's shoulders slumped.

One of the black-coats stepped forward. With the sun behind them, Nash couldn't make out any features. "Good afternoon, Mason. It's been a while."

The woman's accent was distinctly French and yet somehow oddly familiar to Nash's ears.

He looked up and shielded his eyes. The first thing he saw was the Glock 17 Gen 5 FR pointed at his chest. The second was the face of the person who held it. It was a face Nash was well acquainted with.

Nash clenched his eyes shut. "Been a long time." He opened them again and squinted. "You here to kill me?"

Sophia Ocon, Nash's former lover, flicked the safety switch of her pistol. "I've been waiting to do this for a very long time."

CHAPTER
FIVE

Sophia lowered her gun and wrapped her arms around Nash, pulling him into a hug. She nuzzled her nose into the side of his face before giving him a kiss on the check. While holding him in this intimate embrace, she gently removed the Beretta from the back of his jeans and pocketed it before reeling back and slapping him hard across the cheek.

"Anyone else picking up mixed signals here?" Bishop asked.

Eva gave a slight shake of her head. "For once I'm agreeing with your general lack of perceptiveness."

Bishop blinked a few times. "Thank you?"

"We've got a van waiting," Sophia stated cooly. "You three follow Baptiste here and I'll follow you. Remember, we're the ones with guns, so do exactly as we ask. Is that clear?"

Baptiste was the not-waiter who now sported a black eye and a self-satisfied air.

Holding up a finger, Bishop said, "I've always made it a lifelong rule to never follow anyone called Baptiste."

A poke in the back with Sophia's gun put paid to Bishop's half-hearted protest. The group reluctantly headed back the way they'd come. Sophia's team were adept at concealing their weapons while ensuring they were at the ready. They were fortunate that the grey day was keeping the crowds away from the riverside cafes and restaurants.

Nash was too stunned to offer up much in the way of protest. How long had it been since he'd seen Sophia in the flesh? Ten years? More? Her hair was shorter than he remembered, a chocolate brown bob. It suited her. She still looked amazing. Damn those French genes.

"All these black-coats DGSE?" he asked, more to fill the awkward silence than anything.

Sophia shook her head and gave him the slightest of grins. "After all this time, that's the first thing you ask me?"

"It was either that or ask where my black Rolling Stones t-shirt went."

Sophia sniggered. "It fit me better."

Choosing not to respond, primarily because he knew she was right, Nash changed the topic. "If you don't mind me asking a second question, what was the slap for?"

"I promised my past self if I ever saw you again I'd slap you across the face for dumping me. And one should always be true to oneself, wouldn't you agree?"

"I didn't dump you. We mutually agreed to—"

Sophia stopped walking. "You never returned my last few messages, in which I left the door open for us to get back together. Therefore, you dumped me."

"That's a biased view of things. I was simply—"

"Dude," Eva interjected, "she's armed. You're not. Let her have this one."

Nash thrust his hands into his pockets and ascended the stairs without further comment. A light drizzle sprinkled the city, and the scant Melbournians outside darted for cover or produced umbrellas, seemingly from out of nowhere. At the top of the stairs a white commercial van awaited them with another black-coat who slid the door open, a gesture less friendly than it sounded. The grey-haired man opened his coat to reveal a holster and gun, emphasising their lack of options. All three piled into the empty van without protest. Sophia and not-waiter Baptiste with the odd haircut followed them in, guns at the ready in case they had any ideas; luckily for them, Nash didn't. Baptiste reserved a particularly severe sneer for him.

The van took off with a jolt. Eva, Bishop and Nash sprawled backwards on the metal floor, sliding into the rear of the van. They were flung against the side wall when the driver did a sharp U-turn.

Nash's wits were slowly returning as the shock wore off. "How did you find me?"

Given their history, he asked in the singular rather than the plural.

Uncharacteristically, Sophia screwed her face up in hesitancy. "That's not necessarily an easy one to answer."

Nash waited. When nothing further was forthcoming, he pressed, "But there is an answer?"

"Oh, yes. Most assuredly."

The lack of resolution to his simple query dangled between them. Whatever Sophia knew, she was keeping it close to her chest for her own reasons. Assuming further questions on the same subject would receive a similar response, Nash asked a different question.

"Where are we headed, Sophia?"

"Well, there are a couple of ways I could answer that." She slipped her Glock into a shoulder holster. "Nietzsche believed in one simple philosophy: that our destination, our life's raison d'être as it were, is to ultimately become who we really are. That is the destination of one's true self."

Nash's shoulders slumped. "And the other way you could answer?"

Sophia leaned her head to one side. "Are you familiar with Daft Punk's song, 'Around the World'?"

Eva crossed her arms. "Oh, I like her."

Nash squinted. "I'm so glad." He turned back to Sophia. "We're not responsible for the things we've been framed for. They're all Tartarus. We're the ones trying to take them down."

The word Tartarus certainly garnered a reaction. Sophia's eye twitched when he said it. It was a tiny, almost imperceptible movement but Nash noticed. He wasn't sure if it was a grimace or a flinch. Perhaps both—a flimace? Telling her the truth wasn't much of a gamble, he figured. If she worked for Tartarus—something Nash would find hard to believe of Sophia, at least the Sophia he once knew—then she'd already know. If not, he could start to persuade her of the truth. His old self used to be quite good at persuading Sophia Ocon.

"We believe Tartarus are going to stage a terrorist attack and present evidence to suggest they uncovered it alone while every other spy agency was completely unaware. They'll frame it as Tartarus being superior and more agile than the old guard of intelligence organisations. They are going to stage a bloody and public terrorist attack in a self-aggrandising gesture for legitimacy. This is their big play, and they'll kill thousands to do it."

Sophia tapped her knee rhythmically. "The very kinds of acts you and your cohorts here are accused of?"

Nash found it hard to get a read on her. He wanted to believe the woman he once loved would be impervious to the lure of Tartarus, but ten years was a long time. People could change in far less. Hell, Nash was hardly the man Sophia would remember. Did he trust her? Did she trust him? Whose side was she on?

"We didn't do those things, Sophia. Tartarus did. They murdered hundreds in a fishing village and then a mosque, assassinated a CIA data analyst and a member of the British government. They stole from drug cartels with the intention of selling the cocaine on the open market. They're the malevolent ones here, not us. We've just been framed for it."

"It seems to me," she replied evenly, "a guilty man would claim his innocence as vigorously as an innocent one."

Nash exhaled slowly. "Then logic would dictate that evidence to determine one's guilt or innocence should be judged by a wise and impartial party." Nash waited a beat. "Such as yourself."

"You trying to butter me up, Mason Nash?" A wicked grin grossed Sophia's red lips. "Because you've done that to me before."

Eva nudged Nash in the ribs. "Oh, I really like her."

THE PRIVATE JET evened out and sped to parts unknown. Nash, Eva and Bishop sat unrestrained in the back of the plane, while Sophia and her team occupied at the front. They had driven directly to the airport and then to a private hangar, likely used by celebrities, the super-rich and, in this case, foreign intelligence organisations who somehow managed to bypass Australian Customs. They were wheels up an hour and a half after the impromptu reunion with Sophia, leaving Australia and Nash's toothbrush far behind.

Alone for the first time, Eva leaned forward. "Is she Tartarus?"

There was a delicacy to the question. Eva understood the weight it held. Even the normally less-than-emotional Bishop winced at the query.

"I... I don't know."

It was the truth. Nash wanted to believe more than anything that the woman he once loved wouldn't have laid herself at the altar of evil, even if tempted, and would have the moral fortitude to reject all Tartarus stood for. But wanting to believe is not the same as knowing. A lot can happen in ten years. People change for all sorts of reasons. Nash certainly had. Besides, does anyone truly know another? At one time he thought he'd known this woman more than he knew himself. But that was a long time ago.

"Where do you think we're headed?"

"Probably not the opening of the Cannes Film Festival, unfortunately." Seeing Eva and Bishop's humourless faces, Nash answered more seriously. "I assume France, or at least a DGSE rendition site."

"Sounds delightful." Bishop cracked his neck. "Do you think they have room service?"

Ignoring him, Eva touched Nash's knee, her voice softer. "How did you two meet?"

Nash screwed his mouth to the side. "You asking because you care or because you're looking for intelligence to leverage this situation?"

With a *you got me* expression, she replied, "Can't it be a bit of both?"

There was no point being angry at the question; Nash would have asked the same. They were, after all, being held captive by a foreign power. Any information could be advantageous.

"We met in Paris," Nash started. "I was on a job. Paul had righted my course at MI6 and I was once again the golden boy." He shook his head. "I was so much more arrogant back then."

Nash gazed out the window as he told his tale.

THIRTEEN YEARS AGO

THERE WERE many who believed the banks of the Seine to be the most romantic place on Earth.

It was unlikely that Franciszek Andrysiak was one of them, however; at least not at this precise moment. Mainly because of the gun pointed at his forehead. Plus, he'd just soiled himself. Romance probably wasn't on his mind.

Nash's hold on the gun was unwavering. It was a quiet part of the riverbank, especially given the recent rains and the late hour. The bank was slick and dark. The distant thrum of a nightclub echoed from some dark corner of the city.

The rotund little man looked like a stock comedic character from central casting. His plump appearance veiled a more sinister interior. Franciszek was whimpering now, realising his fate and his utter inability to do a damn thing about it.

"I... I have money!" he blubbered in a childlike voice.

He reached into his pocket. Nash allowed it, as he'd already searched him. Dozens of five-hundred-euro banknotes cascaded from his plump hands, spilling onto the wet bricks. Snot dripped from his nose, and tears poured from his reddening eyes.

Responsible for supplying arms to terrorist organisations the world over, Franciszek was tied to at least eighty-seven deaths, likely far more. Bombings in Tokyo, Lisbon and Québec had been traced back to explosives he'd sold. A busload of tourists in Addis Ababa had been destroyed with C4 he'd supplied firsthand. And yet for all his crimes, Franciszek would never see the inside of a jail cell. He'd faced trial twice and both times had been acquitted. Each time, his powerful family had manipulated juries, had the children of jurors threatened and, in at least one instance, raped. They had bribed officials, made evidence disappear, had judge's cars bombed. Franciszek Andrysiak and particularly his brother, Jakub, were not men who believed in the justice system. No, Franciszek would prefer to rip out his own heart with his bare hands than face prison. This man would receive no justice unless it was at the end of a gun.

Mason Nash pulled the trigger.

The echo reverberated around the brickwork on either side of the river, even with the suppressor. He took a moment to watch the lifeless corpse and felt no remorse. He'd seen photos of the atrocities, watched the surveillance footage, heard the harrowing tales of the man's victims. Nash had no illusions as to the man's guilt. The world would be a better place, if only marginally, without Franciszek Andrysiak in it.

Nash was disappointed that there'd been no incriminating evidence when he'd searched Franciszek. He'd hoped to find something, anything on the Andrysiak crime family or information about the whereabouts of Franciszek's brother, the true brains of the operation. Franciszek, in the whole scheme of things, was small fry. It was his brother who Nash was really after. The UK had seven outstanding warrants for his arrest. All they had to do was find him.

Unfortunately, the only phone Franciszek had on him was a non-smart burner phone with three numbers stored in it. Nash doubted it would lead to Jakub, but he pocketed it anyway.

Giving the body a hefty nudge with his foot, the blob of a man rolled into the Seine, landing with a watery plop. It was quickly carried away with the fast-moving flow. Nash figured there was a fifty-fifty chance the body would be identified before it left the confines of the city. It would be seen, even at this hour, but the human mind prefers to suggest alternatives to anything horrific. It wasn't a body, it was a log. Or a mannequin. Anything but a recently executed arms-dealing terrorist.

Straightening his tie, Nash brushed himself off and considered making his way to a little twenty-four-hour bistro in the 11th arrondissement. Inhaling the cold night air, he turned towards the steps.

"That was cold."

Hand diving into his jacket, Nash stopped. The woman wore a long camel-hair coat. She was all warm chocolate brown hair and icy disposition, but that wasn't what stopped Nash from reaching for his gun. It was *her* gun— aimed at his chest. The woman was neither angry nor particularly upset at having witnessed an execution. Her eyes weren't intense, nor were they scared. Even in the low light he could see that her vivid green eyes simply were that: vivid green.

"CIA or MI6?"

Nash blinked several times. "What do you mean?"

The woman smirked. "MI6, then."

Nash had the impression she was a well-practiced smirker, as she was damn good at it.

"You don't seem to be overly concerned a man just died?"

She tilted her head. "Murdered, you mean?"

"Well, I don't know about that," he said while casually searching the bank for any more surprises.

She sighed, but it was more theatrical than out of frustration. "Murder is the unlawful premeditated killing of one human being by another. Now, as France hasn't had an executioner in over forty years and as far as I can tell you're not a representative of the République française, I can only assume what you just did fits the definition of murder. Unless I'm missing something, I'd say you murdered that man, yes?"

Damn. This woman is cool.

"I think man is far too generous a word to use for him."

Not knowing who the woman holding the gun was or what she knew, Nash deliberately didn't use the man's name. Like her, he was playing his cards close to his chest.

"And what would you use instead?" She arched a challenging eyebrow. She was well practiced at that too.

"I think the appropriate term would be," Nash scratched the back of his head, searching for the appropriate phrase, "oxygen thief? Dumpster fire of a human being? A walking talking equivalent of rectal bleeding?"

She laughed. Nash liked her laugh. Though she threw her head back in delight, the gun never moved from him for an instant.

Nash admired her dimples as she said, "Franciszek positively deserved it. The world will not miss his filth, that much I know."

DGSE, for sure.

"Just on the off chance someone was watching, I think it wise we..." Nash motioned to the nearby stairs.

She frowned in agreeance and slipped the gun into her pocket. Her hand remained in her pocket, and the bulge was aimed at Nash. Making to walk off, her other hand flicked to the pile of euros next to where Franciszek's body tumbled into the Seine.

"You just going to leave it there?"

Nash scowled. *Is she proposing taking a terrorist's money?*

"It's blood money. Tainted."

Motioning for Nash to back up, she leaned down and picked up the wad of cash. "The money doesn't care." She gave him a coquettish tilt of her head. "I do."

Motioning with the gun in her pocket, she gestured for Nash to precede her up the stairs. *She's smart*, he thought. A possible thief, but smart.

Reaching street level, the city once again came into focus. Parisians darting from one point to the other, cars jostling for position, even at this hour. The two walked for a while, Nash a couple of metres in front. They approached a woman sleeping rough on carboard. She rested under several multicoloured blankets next to a shopping cart full of plastic bags containing who knew what.

Nash's companion called out to him, "Hold on."

She leaned down and gently touched the woman on the shoulder. Understandably startled at being disturbed in her sleep, the homeless woman recoiled. Holding up a hand to indicate she meant no harm, the DGSE agent spoke soothingly and handed the bundle of euros to the startled woman. When the homeless woman realised what was happening she burst into tears and pulled her benefactor into a fierce bear hug. Overlapping thank yous cascaded from her chapped lips as her hands repeatedly thumped the woman's back.

Extracting herself and wishing the still-crying woman well, Nash's new companion glowed as they walked away.

He shook his head good-naturedly. "A DGSE agent with a heart. Wonders never cease."

"Why do you think I'm DGSE?" she asked in a way that completely confirmed Nash's suspicions.

"Aren't you wondering what she's going to do with her newfound wealth?"

"No." She shook her head. "I'm more concerned with what I'm going to do with you."

"You could buy me a drink?" Nash suggested.

There was that smirk again. "My, quite forward, aren't you?"

"Sometimes. But I'm also something else."

"What's that?"

"Thirsty. Hence the drink, you see."

The woman's forehead creased as if she were contemplating the idea. "What's your name?"

"Mason Nash. And yours?"

"Sophia." She extracted her gun hand from her coat and extended it to Nash. "Sophia Ocon."

As it turned out, Sophia Ocon was indeed DGSE and had followed the same Interpol lead Nash had been chasing for weeks. Nash just got there first.

They sat in the tiny all-night café, huddled around a small table mere hours before dawn. Clumps of young people piled out of nightclubs arm in arm, singing and shouting in joyous spirit.

The waiter brought them a second round of cheese and

left to serve a newly arrived group of nightclubbers in bright skimpy attire. Despite being four in the morning, the place was pumping. Sophia was excellent company. Quick to laugh and even quicker to smile, she had charm to spare.

Nash spun Franciszek's phone in his fingers.

Noticing his distraction, Sophia asked, "Considering ordering a pizza? I know a good place."

"I have no doubt." Nash stopped spinning the device and placed it on the table between them. "Franciszek was only a cog in the Andrysiaks' web..."

"How can you have a cog in a web?" Sophia waved her Roquefort about. "It doesn't make sense."

Ignoring her, Nash continued. "His brother Jakub is the driver of it all. Always has been. He's the brains of the operation. I searched Franciszek for any evidence but this was all he had."

"What are you going to do," she asked, amused, "give Jakub a call and ask him to dinner?"

"Dinner?" Nash tapped the phone. "Not dinner. No."

He looked her dead in the eye, daring her to say something.

"Look," her words tumbled out slowly, "I'm already in breach of at least a half dozen protocols by not dragging you to the local authorities."

"You've sat here for twenty minutes complaining about how the brothers have been able to get away with so many crimes, and how if only more had stood up to stop them it would have alleviated so much pain and misery in the world. Jakub is a terrorist. He's sold arms to both sides in Somalia, the Boko Haram insurgency and countless others. He's ordered the murders of UN peacekeepers, bombed embassies and killed any official who had the audacity to want him held accountable for his crimes. He's murdered, raped and terrorised." Nash held up the phone. "What if we have the power to end his tyranny once and for all?"

Sophia leaned back in her chair. Nash was sure the arch in her back and the heave of her chest were deliberate.

"What are you proposing?"

"We see who answers the numbers saved in this phone," he said, fluttering his eyelids, as innocent as a newborn fawn. "Nothing more."

"Going rogue like that, even to take down someone as vile as Jakub Andrysiak..." Sophia squinted. "You're going to lead me astray, aren't you, Mason Nash?"

"I get the impression you only go to places of your choosing, Sophia Ocon."

Her tight red lips turned upward in a flirtatious smirk, then she shook her head defeatedly. "You'll be the death of me. What's the play?"

Once she'd heard it, Sophia let out a low whistle. "You are a risk taker, aren't you?" Her eyes drifted outside, but it was clear it wasn't the street scene that was occupying her thoughts.

"My organisation expressly forbade me from taking Jakub Andrysiak on," she twirled her hair, "unless it is in direct ` connection to an active investigation." She lifted an eyebrow. "Seems I've found a man who qualifies."

"You wouldn't be using me to get to him, would you?" Nash asked.

She cast him a *c'est la vie* expression. "I'd say we're using one another for mutually beneficial outcomes, no?"

Minutes later the two of them were crowded in a tiny phone booth in the back of the café. Once used for payphone calls, it now hosted mobile phone calls in a quieter environment, away from street noise. Sophia's body was pressed against his in the small confines. Neither seemed troubled by the proximity. Nash certainly wasn't. Her Chanel Nº5 was intoxicating.

"It's a bit tight," Nash observed.

"Not the first time I've heard that," Sophia answered with lashings of self-assuredness.

Not helping.

Forcing himself to concentrate on the matter at hand, Nash hit the first number in the phone and waited. Sophia pressed her ear against his hand to listen. The call was answered on the second ring.

"Allo?"

"We have Franciszek," Nash stated evenly in English.

He held his breath. There was an elongated pause.

"Let me speak to him."

"No."

"No?" the voice at the other end asked in anger. "Do you have any idea who you are speaking to?"

Nash did. It was unmistakably Jakub.

"I do. But you have no idea who you're speaking to, or what we're capable of."

Sophia leaned back and arranged her impressive features into an impressed look. Nash went on.

"Your brother was flagged by Interpol as having been spotted in the Latin Quarter. A rather populous part of the city for a wanted man to be frequenting, one would have thought. Every law enforcement agency in the country wants your brother; we happened to get to him first. We think we deserve some sort of recompense for keeping him out of their hands, wouldn't you say?"

"If you hurt my brother I'll—"

"Save the threats. This isn't a Hollywood movie. He's fine," Nash lied, "but it will only remain so if you follow my instructions very closely. Do we have an accord?"

Nash could virtually hear the gnashing of teeth through the phone.

"State your demands."

THREE HOURS LATER, Sophia and Nash watched the pre-dawn light spread across the grey Paris architecture as they sat on the lower steps of the Basilica of Sacré-Cœur in Montmartre. The view of the awakening city was spectacular. In the cold, they huddled as close as lovers. It was Paris, after all.

Only a few souls braved the chill to watch Paris come alive from the most beautiful vantage point in the city. On the steps, two small clumps of people sat with phones at the ready, eager to capture a moment to post for the folks back home.

A large American town car rolled slowly into the forecourt of the Sacré-Cœur. It was a dead-end street leading to a small cul-de-sac at the end. They drove slowly, ominously.

In a low voice, Sophia asked, "Is this plan going to work?"

Nash gave her a reassuring squeeze. "There's an old military dictum." Her face turned to his, her eyes tired but expectant. "If we don't know what we're doing, the enemy certainly can't anticipate our future actions."

Her face crumpled into concern. "I thought you were going to give me some reassuringly sage advice."

"I think we've known each other long enough—"

"Eight hours?"

"—that we don't sugar coat things. This could go pear-shaped in an instant. We need to be ready."

She planted her fists on her hips. "Not exactly inspiring."

"If you want inspiring, read Martin Luther King Junior. If you want someone who gets things done, usually with punching and gunplay and the occasional explosion, call Mason Nash."

"A little better, I guess." Her face snapped into seriousness. "We're on."

The driver's side door of the town car opened and a hulk of a man in a white skivvy stepped out. Draped in gold chains and attitude, he was the personification of a gym junkie. He opened the passenger side door and Jakub Andrysiak stepped out.

Where Jakub's brother had an amusing plump exterior, his older sibling was diametrically the opposite. Bulked from hours in the gym and likely steroids, his thick black beard and razor-sharp designer fuckboy haircut gave him a menacing presence. The two other bodyguards who exited the car added to the aesthetic.

Jakub scanned the steps, searching for the person who'd kidnapped his brother. Nash stood, gave him a friendly wave like a Forrest Gump meme and called out, "Yoohoo!"

"Are you *trying* to piss him off?" Sophia asked in a low voice.

"A little, yeah."

"Marvellous."

Nash descended the stairs towards the crime lord and his intimidating bodyguards, with Sophia close behind.

When they reached Jakub, the big man scowled.

"What's your name?"

"Why?"

The big man's eye twitched; he clearly wasn't used to

people questioning him. He lowered his head menacingly. "Because I always like to know the names of those I kill."

"You kill me and your brother won't live past dawn."

"I asked your name. Give it to me."

"Skyscraper. Broccoli Skyscraper."

Jakub's lips parted in astonishment, as if he'd never been mocked in his life. His eyes swivelled to Sophia inquiringly.

"I'm his associate," Sophia added, smiling wide, "Chlamydia Trenchcoat. Pleased to meet you."

Unable to help himself, Nash laughed. The woman was whip smart and matched him perfectly. Jakub wasn't as amused. Nash could actually see his teeth grind. His bodyguards slowly circled them, cutting off any escape.

"You claim to have my brother?"

"Correct."

"That's interesting." Jakub rubbed his hand across his beard. "Because my brother washed up near the La Seine Musicale an hour ago."

"Ah."

Jakub and his entire crew extracted pistols and aimed them at the pair.

The crime lord shook his head with a frightening leer. "I have the best torturers in the world. We're gonna keep you in agony for weeks, my friend. You're going to experience pain like you've never..."

Jakub's voice trailed off. Instead of recoiling in fear, Nash had simply hefted his eyebrows and rocked on his heels. His utter lack of concern about being exposed, the threat of torture and the sight of guns perplexed Jakub to the point of distraction.

The big man blinked several times. "Did... did you not hear what I said?"

"Oh, I did," Nash replied jovially. "Now you hear to what I have to say, very closely." He leaned in close to Jakub. "Lemongrass."

Before the crime lord could react, every one of the many people who occupied the steps of Sacré-Cœur leapt up and aimed pistols and carbines at the bodyguards, having been concealed under blankets and in camera bags. There were seventeen in total. At the far end of the road, police cars with flashing lights cut off the only exit. Uniformed police scrambled from their hidden alcoves, service revolvers at the ready.

Distracted by the sudden movement, Jacob and his goons wheeled in surprise. Sophia leapt forward, grasping Jakub's gun hand and forcing it down while bringing her own pistol to the side of his head.

"Drop it or your brains get blown out to Sarcelles." She pressed the barrel hard into his temple to emphasise the point. "Now!"

The bodyguards glared at their boss until he gave a reluctant nod. The clatter of weaponry on the ground was immediately followed by running footsteps. The police quickly ushered the criminals into waiting police vans.

It had been Sophia's idea. In the space of a few short hours she'd brought her organisation up to speed, leaving out the detail of Franciszek's assassination, and explaining how they'd orchestrated a rendezvous with the wanted Jakub Andrysiak. Her superiors had no choice but to comply, and organise local law enforcement.

Watching the cursing criminals being carted away, Nash asked, "Why lemongrass?"

"Excuse me?"

"Why was lemongrass the codeword?"

"Ah, well, I thought it's unlikely to come up in conversation with an arms dealing terrorist." She beamed. "Plus, I've got a hankering for Thai food." She seductively placed her chin to her shoulder. "Care to join me?"

"It's a bit early for Thai, isn't it?"

"Oh, I'm confident we'll find a way to entertain ourselves until dinner," her shoulder bumped his playfully, "or my name isn't Chlamydia Trenchcoat."

"Damn." Eva shook her head. "After meeting like that I'd have slept with her."

"Really?" Bishop placed a fist under his chin. "Tell me more. Don't leave anything out." When she ignored him, Bishop turned to Nash. "Seems the woman holds a gun on you pretty frequently. When you first met, today. Something of a habit?" He straightened his back. "Not sure it's entirely healthy."

Eva shook her head. "Says the man who wants to shoot firearms while we're having sex." Like Bishop, she turned her attention to Nash. "And now she's back after all these years."

Not immediately responding, Nash's eyes drifted to the front of the plane where Sophia was huddled with her DGSE compatriots.

"Yes. And I have to wonder why." He exhaled slowly. "And who she's truly working for."

CHAPTER
SIX

Nash told Sophia everything.

Officious in her business suit, she'd finished her huddle with her colleagues. She effortlessly ordered the men around. They didn't cower like she was an ogre, nor did they slavenly mope about in reluctant compliance. Instead, they snapped to her requests with respect, deferring to her intelligence and experience. *As they should,* Nash said to himself.

Sophia had requested a private "chat". That was far too casual a term for such a demand. Ignoring Eva and Bishop's raised eyebrows, Sophia led Nash to the front of the private jet and he laid everything out. From the assassins sent after him at Devil's End to their South American takedown of a Tartarus outpost to the clash with Pinchot's henchmen in Seoul to the confrontation with Paul's father in a barn outside of Paris, he left nothing out. If she really was Tartarus—he wasn't convinced either way just yet—she would know it all. If not, there was a chance, however slight, she may be able to help them, perhaps even let them go.

Nash had learned long ago not to pin his hopes to such things, but Sophia infused him with optimism. *And that's why she'll be your downfall.* Nash wasn't sure where the thought came from, but he was equally certain he didn't want to give it air to breathe.

For a full minute she steepled her fingers and uttered no sound. Nash knew well enough not to interrupt Sophia when she was ensconced in one of her deep ruminations. The woman could concentrate on a subject for hours until she came to the right course of action.

Finally, she tapped her steepled fingers on her chin. "So, you think Pinchot is the key to unlocking Tartarus?"

There was something in the way she asked the question that struck Nash as odd. It had been years since they'd talked, but he still could read her. Or at least, he thought he could. Her faux casual question struck Nash as loaded.

"Yes. We think he may still be in France. That's where we were headed next." Nash eyed the back of the plane, where Eva and Bishop were doing their best not to stare. "Although we were hoping it would be more voluntary than the current circumstances." Nash laid on the charm that had once been so effective with Sophia. "If you could see your way to letting us go in France, I give you my word we'll keep you up to date with what we find."

It was the longest of long shots, but Nash had nothing left to lose.

"No." Sophia said resolutely.

"No?"

"We won't be doing that, Mason."

Nash shifted uncomfortably in his seat. "Then can you at least help us find Pinchot?"

Resting her hands in her lap, seemingly enjoying his discomfort, Sophia replied, "Also no."

It appeared Nash's charm wasn't anywhere near as potent as it had once been.

"We're not going to help you find Pinchot," Sophia tilted her head. "We're also not going to France."

There was the slightest dance of amusement in her features, which only confounded him. Her words were belligerent, but her eyes entertained.

Nash's eyes narrowed. "Where are we headed, Sophia?"

"Let me answer the next question you're going to ask along with that one."

"The next question?"

"He's in New York."

"Who is?"

"Pinchot," Sophia replied. "That's why we're flying there now."

"I'm confused."

She tapped his knee. "Not an uncommon state for you."

Nash's mind reeled. He still didn't know how Sophia had found them. Now she was telling him not only did she already know about Pinchot but she had somehow tracked him down. It was too much to take in, and a lot of it didn't ring true. As Nash sat across from Sophia the ripples of unease multiplied and swept across him like waves. She stood and left him with a condescending pat on the shoulder and a teetering pile of unanswered questions.

For the remaining twenty odd hours of the flight, Sophia hardly spoke to Nash directly. In fact, she did her best to avoid any one-on-one interaction. They all slept as much as they could, had a few group discussions, but Sophia spent most of the time either speaking with her team or huddled over her laptop.

Why was she avoiding Nash? Was it because she was still making her mind up about him and his stories about

Pinchot? Did she not want to impinge on the inevitable interrogation to come? Was she reluctant to talk for too long in fear of rekindling a fragment of what they'd once had? Was it because he was now her enemy and she didn't want to be caught out? Nash didn't know, and the lack of knowing only increased the ambiguity of their plight.

He only had part of the story, and it was driving him crazy.

THE PRIVATE JET landed at JFK just after seven am. They were bundled into a minivan and rushed through the city—well, as much as one can rush anywhere in New York traffic.

All these hours later, the revelation about Pinchot was still shocking. Jack Pinchot was ex-CIA, New York was his home turf—so how had Sophia's team managed to find him so quickly? Were they already hunting him? Were they on the same side?

As far as Nash could guess, the DGSE safe house was in an expensively gentrified and leafy part of the city. Somewhere in Brooklyn, he thought, perhaps Fort Greene or Carroll Gardens. It was a nice part of the city, but he doubted they'd come all this way for a cream cheese bagel and a stroll.

Shown into a townhouse on a quiet but affluent street, the three were escorted to separate rooms, each with an en suite, a change of clothes and barred windows. Nash showered, changed and waited. He didn't have to wait long.

The knock was polite, practically timid. He didn't answer immediately. It was important not to appear too eager, too amenable. After the second knock he said, "Come in."

Like Nash, Sophia had freshened up and changed.

Unlike Nash, she was stunning. How the woman made blue jeans and a simple white shirt seem demure and sexy at the same time was beyond him. She slunk into the room and sat at the end of the bed next to him. Nash wasn't sure if the positioning was deliberate or not.

All the old memories came flooding back. The passionate arguments—she'd wanted him to leave MI6 but Nash couldn't. That was before Nash's own doubts had crept in. Later in his career he would have relented. Or perhaps Sophia had planted the doubts, and it had taken him too long to realise she'd been right all along. By then it was too late, she'd already disappeared from his life and he'd never see her again. Or so he'd thought.

"Been run off my feet all day." Her palms slid down her jeans.

"Kidnappings always keep you busier than you expect." He'd attempted to sound witty, but the edge was sharper than anticipated.

Sophia noticed, and chose her words carefully. "I prefer to call it an involuntary reunion."

Her own attempt at levity fell flat, causing her to shuffle awkwardly. Sophia was softer now than she'd been on the plane, less officious. It may have been because she no longer had the underlings about her, but Nash sensed there was something else.

"How did you find us, Sophia? Me?" It wasn't idle curiosity; Nash was still trying to piece it all together.

"The master spy wants to know where he went wrong?"

"It's more than that, and you know it." He slapped on the charm, though he wasn't sure she bought it. "We're trying to save the world here, and our respective organisations."

"Former." She held up a well-manicured finger. "Your *former* organisation."

Nash had to concede the point. "They're compromised and they don't even know it, or if they do, they're terrified to do anything about it for fear they'll talk to the wrong person and become the next victim. Asking how we were discovered is not vanity, Soph," Nash realised it was the first time in years he'd used his affectionate name for her, "it's about survival. Knowing how you found us tells us a great many things."

"Like who I'm working for?"

Feeling his mouth twitch, Nash chose not to answer. "You owe me that much."

"I don't owe you anything."

"A Rolling Stones t-shirt at least."

Sophia's lips pursed. "My superiors put me on the case. Somehow, they were aware of us, seems they always knew. They said I understood you better than anyone and that would somehow help find you wherever you were hiding in the world. The first place I looked was where we'd spent most of our time together, but after an exhaustive search I determined you weren't in my bedroom." The renewed attempt at humour falling flat once more seemed to urge her on. "I was assigned various teams, one of which comprised our ace data analysts. They were assigned hefty server and satellite time to run all sorts of facial recognition and profiling searches. They were the ones who found you in Pakistan. That's when I jumped on a plane. They picked you up again in Singapore. Nice job with the switching profiles and appearances, it almost worked, but AI can counter those sorts of things now."

That didn't tell Nash an awful lot. The IT person could have been Tartarus, or someone could have planted it for them to find. He rubbed his temples. All this doublethink wasn't helping his jetlag.

"How did you know about the wine bar? Your man was in place before we even got there."

There was no hiding the self-satisfaction on her face. "We had a woman on the ground when you landed. The moment you turned on your mobile phone in baggage claim she spoofed it, cracked it open like an egg. We saw all the websites you'd visited and how long you'd spent on them. The IT bods then took a data dump and trawled for key phrases and anything not related to *My Little Pony*." She studied his reaction. She knew the site where he and his group exchanged what he'd thought up until this moment were private messages. "We made the owner of the bar an enormous offer to let us have the place for a few hours and here we are."

It was plausible enough, but it didn't exactly answer his questions. Nash needed more.

"How did you find Pinchot?" He shook his head. "Scratch that. How did you know about Pinchot to begin with?"

Her eyes distant, she spoke slowly. "Before I was assigned to find you, my superior Juliette had tasked me to help, uh, root Tartarus out of the DGSE."

"Surely there's an internal affairs department? One that—"

"We believe they were the first department Tartarus compromised."

"Ah."

"I think that was the real reason Juliette assigned me to go find you. We wanted to get to you first. There's no way you and your little cohort could have done what they framed you for. Plus, if you were the good guys then we needed to find out what you knew. She sent me, out of everyone at the DGSE, because she couldn't be sure of anyone else."

"Why was she so sure of you?" Nash wasn't certain why he asked the question, but it seemed important.

"Because we were once lovers." Sophia studied Nash's face, searching for a reaction.

"That'd do it."

"That's all you have to say?"

"About you being bi?" Nash raised a quizzical palm. "I'm not going to dismiss it as unimportant, because it isn't, but I think you know me well enough to know I support you and I'm glad you found out. I hope she made you happy."

The revelation, while a surprise of sorts, wasn't entirely shocking either. Like Nash, Sophia had always been an admirer of the female form, its infinite varieties and qualities. He recalled their lamentations about fellow workers who failed to support equality for their LGBTQIA+ compatriots. He meant what he said, he hoped Sophia realising her sexuality had brought her happiness, as that's all he'd ever wished for her.

"She did make me happy," her face was raked with a veil of sadness, "until she didn't. We were better friends in the end." Sophia folded her arms. "Why did you assume bi and not lesbian?"

Nash shrugged. "Market research."

It was the first time in years Nash had heard Sophia's laugh, and he instantly realised how much he'd missed it. Never a shallow fake one, you had to earn it, which made you appreciate it even more. It was a full-throated guffaw.

"Tu es un imbécile." She exhaled heavily as if a weight had been lifted.

"Are there any other life-altering truth bombs you want to drop?"

Her levity evaporated in an instant, and her face grew paler by the second. She swallowed several times. There was a lot more at play than Nash realised.

Finally regaining the ability to speak, she said, "You were asking about Pinchot?"

Reclaiming her composure, Sophia explained how Pinchot intersected Nash's story at multiple points. First the CIA and MI6 were after him after the Tartarus compound raid in Puerto Rico. Then again at Seoul, where the story had suddenly morphed into Nash's Scooby gang attacking an innocent Pinchot for vague and implausible reasons. Then again in Paris, where Nash and his cohort had suddenly become drug dealers. According to Sophia, the framing of Nash, Eva, Bishop and the rest never rang true for her. And if they weren't responsible, she postulated, then who was?

"Pinchot seemed like a likely candidate," she said.

"Smart."

"I like to think so." Sophia rubbed an imaginary badge on her lapel. "I had my team investigate his finances. The CIA pays well, but not buying-multiple-Lamborghinis-in-your-retirement well. That and the yachts and luxury apartments around the world. It was blatant, almost—"

"Arrogant?" Nash interrupted. "That's Pinchot to a tee."

Sophia bobbed her head in agreement. "So, we started seeking out the poor hard-done-by ex-CIA golden child, but he'd suddenly disappeared. Thanks to what you just told me, I now know why: Cavendish is trying to kill the man who'd essentially been running Tartarus and doing such a poor job of it. It all makes sense now."

"But you found him?"

"Back to those boffins again, yes. All the resources they'd assigned me to find you, I surreptitiously redirected to search for Pinchot. We had the server farm and satellites and access to bleeding edge facial recognition and profiling searches, so why not use them? I just didn't tell my superiors who or what we were searching for. Technically I was still searching for you, so I was still doing as ordered. The same search techniques that nabbed you gave us a flag not long after Pinchot was in transit and heading for the US. He's holed up three blocks from here."

"What are you planning to do?" Nash stood up. "Can I get to him?"

Pushing her palms down in a calming motion, Sophia didn't even try to hide her amusement. "We move tonight. This is off the books, obviously. Not only did I not get approval to trace him, Pinchot's a US citizen within his own borders and with no red notices against his name. My team have to do this one clinically clean or else we'll receive career enemas and likely serious jail time."

"A career enema?" Nash chuckled. "That's a line Eva would use."

"You like her."

It was more a statement than a question.

"She's damn good at what she does. They both are, far better than I was at their age. They're in a new relationship, but I've never seen it impinge on their professionalism. They're some of the best spies I've ever seen." He inclined his head in her direction. "And I've seen some brilliant spies in my time."

Nash wasn't sure why he had to emphasise their relationship, but he felt compelled to.

Sophia shouldered him playfully. "I wasn't suggesting you were sleeping with her, Mason, but I certainly wouldn't blame you if you were. It was more that I saw how protective you were of her on the plane, and when we captured you. You two have a bond, that much is obvious. I'm not saying you don't with Bishop..." She paused. "Don't you think it odd everyone refers to him by his last name, even his girlfriend?"

"A little." Feeling they'd strayed too far from the subject at hand, Nash thought it best to refocus. "This operation you have with Pinchot, do you have room for any more?"

The amusement returned to her eyes, but she didn't reply. Nash pressed on.

"If you schedule my interrogation between then and now, I'm sure we can clear up any questions you have."

The word "interrogation" caused her to raise an eyebrow. "This is it."

"It is?" Nash shook his head, confused. "I was expecting some claustrophobic white room with two-way glass, not a quaint bedroom overlooking a park."

"You never had a problem with us being in a bedroom before."

Nash pursed his lips. "Not yet."

"Pardon?" she asked.

"We're not there yet, the old flirt and response."

"Sorry." She wrung her hands. "Old habits and all that." She ran both hands through her hair. "You're a prick, you know?"

"Can we go back to the flirting?"

"You're one of the most wanted men on the planet, I've lost count of the emails, briefings and bulletins I've seen with your stupid face on them."

"Thank you?"

"My superiors grilled me for months on what I knew

about you. They wanted to know everything, and I mean *everything*."

Nash jacked an eyebrow. "Everything?"

She waved a dismissive hand. "Of course, I didn't tell them everything. I left out your inability to hit the high notes when doing the karaoke version of 'Don't Go Breaking My Heart' or your appalling taste in breakfast spreads or your appreciation of expensive stilettos and corsets."

And we're back to the flirting. Nash was getting whiplash.

She continued, her gaze drifting into the middle distance. "Get some rest. Planning starts at twenty-two hundred. We'll move out at oh two hundred."

She stood and proceeded to the door, but suddenly stopped and remained in the centre of the room, seemingly unsure of herself. She took a step towards the door, stopped and turned back, took a step towards Nash, then stopped again. He didn't want to interrupt whatever inner turmoil was going on.

Exhaling loudly, Sophia walked back to Nash and took her phone from her pocket. She gulped, her face ashen but soft.

"Do you want to see a picture of our daughter?"

CHAPTER
SEVEN

N
ash should have slept, but couldn't.

His mind was too busy flipping from shocked to pissed to longing to anger to wonder and back to shocked again.

I'm a father. It was a statement he thought he'd never say. The disbelief was too strong for him to fully appreciate what the revelation meant in any practical sense.

Sabine was ten years old and apparently brilliant. A gifted student, she was also a talented artist and musician, although Nash was sure there was some parental bias on Sophia's behalf. The photos showed a smiling, fun-loving child with mischief in her eyes—eyes that looked uncannily like Nash's.

The likeness was unmistakable. Sabine had his eyes and ears; thankfully she'd inherited her mother's strong jawline, flawless skin and cheekbones. She truly was an amalgam of the two of them, yet was entirely herself. She hadn't inherited her arts inclination from either parent, though the rebellious streak was one Nash and Sophia knew all too well.

His first question was why Sophia had kept her pregnancy from him. He'd asked, strangled with emotion, why she'd never once contacted him. Sophia's reply was a mixture of cliches and choked back tears. She didn't want to burden Nash with a child they hadn't planned for. They'd broken up, and she didn't want to force him back with her choice to have the child. She was at a time in her life where she didn't have many childbearing years left and couldn't risk trying to find another man in that time, so decided to go it alone. She hadn't told Nash due to a mixture of respect and selfishness. Whether to believe her was yet another paradox he'd wrestled with throughout the day.

In readiness for the raid to snatch Pinchot, they had all been told to sleep. Instead, Nash had carved a path on the floor with relentless pacing. So many thoughts piled on top of one another he found it impossible to keep up, let alone make sense of any of them. Though one thought stopped his pacing and made him sit down as his head swum.

The Nash line would no longer end with him. It would live on.

He placed both hands on the bed beside him to retain his balance. The idea of being responsible for the termination of the famed Nash lineage had slowly crept up on him over the last few years. The suddenness of the realisation that this would no longer be the case was yet another on the increasing list of swirling thoughts Nash had to deal with.

The knock on the door made him jump. He checked his watch. Twenty-two hundred hours. It was time to plan the extraction of Pinchot. It felt like barely an hour since Sophia had shocked him with the news of Sabine, but in reality, it had been over twelve.

"Coming."

In a daze, he made his way to the back of the townhouse where his compatriots and the four DGSE agents sat in a modern kitchen and dining area. Everyone but Sophia was huddled around the large dining room table as Sophia made herself a cup of tea in the kitchen.

Her sheepish eyes were wide but hesitantly expectant, seemingly begging him to forgive her betrayal. He gave her a curt greeting devoid of any hint of affection. Sophia made her way to the table and was distracted by a question from her team member, Baptiste.

Eva grasped his forearm, concern etched in her features. "What's wrong?"

Nash wouldn't be surprised if he appeared shell-shocked, and Eva had clearly picked up on it. "I'll tell you later." He patted her hand.

The look of concern on her face didn't dissipate; in fact, it doubled down. Before she had the chance to say anything further, Sophia strode to the front of the room and the chatter stilled. Nash had to concede she knew how to control a room.

"The target is still holed up in the rented townhouse," Sophia advised. "As soon as we arrived in New York, Alain here set up cameras covering Pinchot's place. In the past twelve hours he's only received one grocery delivery. No visitors. No one else has passed a window. As far as we can tell, he's alone."

"That's an awfully big assumption." Bishop stroked his moustache. "So, you're saying the only intelligence we have is less than twenty-four hours old? Nothing before? Who's to say who else is in there? For all we know there could be a bunch of angry groundhogs or Napoleon's Imperial Guard waiting inside. You expect us to rush in and hope for the best?"

Instead of anger at Bishop's questioning, Sophia replied, "Essentially, yes."

She explained the plan. Once finished, Bishop leaned back and crossed his arms. "That could work."

"That's quite the compliment from the strategist of the group," Sophia replied.

Bishop positively beamed until he received an elbow in the ribs from Eva. "Down, boy."

The DGSE team consisted of Sophia, Baptiste the not-waiter, Alain and Claude. Thankfully, Baptiste had managed to quell the flamboyant hair he'd had on display at the wine bar. It turned out he'd worked for his father's winery as a teen and was therefore deemed the best choice to pose as a waiter. In reality, he was the team's armourer and demolitions expert. The grey-haired Alain was the logistics man and scrounger. The beefiest was Claude, the team's muscle, who claimed to have trained with the Russian Spetsnaz, US Green Berets and British SAS. Given the size of his immense shoulders, the thickness of his neck and the way he held himself with various weapons, Nash wasn't about to call him a liar.

Sophia did her best not to come too close or engage Nash in one-on-one conversation. He wasn't sure it was to allow him space to come to terms with his sudden parenthood or to avoid confrontation over her having deceived him for a decade. Either way, it was unfamiliar for Nash to feel uneasy in Sophia's presence.

To help keep himself sane he dove headfirst into planning. Pinchot was situated in a townhouse on Washington Park across from Fort Greene Park. They would hit early in the morning, and spent the next few hours devising various methods of ingress and contingencies. From their own surveillance photos, real estate listings and whatever else

Alain had managed to find online, the layout was relatively straightforward, but it would be close quarters fighting should they encounter resistance.

As it neared midnight they called a break and the teams broke off to eat and chat. In a far corner of the back room, Bishop, Eva and Nash sat huddled eating sandwiches and drinking stale coffee.

"What's going on, Nash?" Eva asked with less humour than usual. "You and Sophia were getting chummy again and now you're frostier than Rudolph the red-nosed reindeer's nut sack. What gives?"

"It's a..." he glanced back in Sophia's direction, "very long story. Let's get through this and then I'll tell you everything."

She held his gaze, seemingly accepting his answer for now. "Should we trust them? They've gone from kidnapping us to buddy buddy pretty quickly."

"If they wanted us dead I think there are easier ways than some elaborate raid," Bishop suggested before stuffing half a sandwich in his mouth. "They could as easily have thrown us out the plane over the Pacific."

Nash tapped his thumb on his beard, accepting the statement. His thoughts once again turned to Pinchot. "Why New York?"

"Sorry?" Eva asked.

"Why New York? If he wants to hide out then why pick one of the most populous cities in the world with millions of cameras pointed in all directions?"

Bishop raised his coffee cup toward Nash. "You tried to live in a remote shitty little town off the beaten track in Nepal and it didn't exactly work out for you." There wasn't maliciousness in Bishop's tone, just matter-of-factness.

"Maybe he knows this turf better. Home ground advantage and whatnot."

It was plausible but it didn't exactly ring true for Nash. He was overlooking something vital and it gnawed at his insides. *What am I missing?*

"Cavendish," Nash said out loud.

"What?"

"Harry said on the conference call Cavendish was in New York. That can't be a coincidence."

"Agreed, but what does it mean?"

Nash huffed. "I don't know."

Before they knew it, the time came for them to roll out. They packed their weapons, night-vision goggles and breaching gear and piled into a waiting van driven by Alain. The three blocks were traversed in silence, the usual state before any operation. Post-raid was the time for bravado and back-slapping, before is when you focus and go through every step in your head until it's as natural as blinking.

Sophia and Baptiste were tasked with cutting the power and covering the rear of the townhouse should Pinchot make a run for it. Claude and Bishop were the breaching team; they'd burst through the front door and head straight for the upstairs bedroom, the likeliest place they'd find Pinchot at two am. Eva and Nash would follow, focusing on sweeping the ground floor. Alain would remain outside with the engine running as backup if anything went wrong.

The windows in the van misted with condensation from their collective breathing. Bishop checked his weapons, inspiring the rest to do the same. Safeties came off and masks went on.

This raid would break so many local and international laws, they could take no chances. Tensions rose in the confined space. The team was as expert as one could hope for, but the mission still felt off. Where did Cavendish fit into things? Why was Pinchot here? Had he allowed himself to be found? Was this all an elaborate trap, and if so, why?

Nash shook his head and pulled out the Desert Eagle Alain had given him and flicked off the safety. Taking a few deep inhales, he was ready.

The van's door slid open silently and Sophia and Baptiste surged out. They didn't glance back as they disappeared down a side street. *There goes the mother of my child,* Nash thought in a momentary daze. He still hadn't fully accepted the concept. He couldn't afford the distraction, and instead focused on checking his ammunition spares.

Alain didn't wait; he took off. After rounding two corners he brought the van to a halt a few houses away and focused on his watch, counting down the seconds. After the requisite three minutes, Alain turned to them and simply said, "Go."

Bishop and Claude leapt wordlessly from the van with Eva and Nash close behind. The street was quiet and not a soul could be seen. The streetlights were few and far between, so the dark shadows were both welcomed and offered an opportunity for enemies to lay in wait.

Bounding up the front steps of the late nineteenth-century townhouse, Bishop covered Claude as he used a lock pick gun to attack the sole keyhole. Within seconds he twisted the doorknob and was in.

This is too easy.

Nash's unease only grew as he and Eva followed the pair through the breach. Claude and Bishop vaulted up the stairs as Eva and Nash peeled left into the downstairs living spaces. Flipping on his night-vision goggles, Nash swept his pistol around the nicely appointed but not overly special lounge room. A door under the stairs led to the basement. He gave two sharp points and Eva executed her assignment. She was through the door and descending the stairs within seconds.

Nash stepped around the corners of the room, where it was less likely he'd encounter a creaking floorboard. His gun swept left to right, finding nothing out of the ordinary. He made his way back into the hall and to the rear of the ground floor, where the kitchen was located. The lack of gunfire from upstairs was encouraging. He moved slowly but methodically. Entering the kitchen, he stopped dead.

In the centre of the floor lay a body.

Male, indeterminate age. Tied to a kitchen chair, both he and the chair were on their side. On the kitchen table were various implements: scalpels, butcher's knives, a hammer. The body was utterly motionless on the floor. Even after a subtle kick with his foot it remained unmoved. Alive ones usually take offence; the dead ones tend to remain indifferent.

Swinging around, Nash checked for any other corpses. Finding none, he leaned down to the body and checked for a pulse. There was none. The body was cool to the touch, but wasn't stone cold, despite the chilly night. Nash estimated death had been in the last hour or so.

Nash checked the man's face; he didn't know him. There were no visible signs of the cause of death, no head-shots or stab wounds. In the harsh green light of the night-vision goggles the man seemed vaguely Middle Eastern in appearance. Whoever this was, they weren't a threat now. Nash rose and returned to the hall.

Eva stepped from the basement door, gun at the ready. Using a sharp hand signals, Nash indicated their next target. Situated between the kitchen and lounge there was only one remaining room on the ground floor. Nash stepped in first with Eva behind him. The room was lined with bookshelves, with a desk at the far end. The high-backed chair faced the rear of the room.

In an instant, Nash was on edge. He turned to Eva; she sensed it too.

As a spy, you develop certain instincts, and if you don't, you soon find yourself at the wrong end of a bullet.

They weren't the only ones in the room.

Creeping forward as stealthily as possible, Eva and Nash took paths to either side of the desk. Nash's intuition was accurate. There was someone sitting in the chair.

Placing his Desert Eagle to the man's head didn't garner a reaction.

"Took you long enough." Jack Pinchot finally turned his head and smiled. "It's been a while, Mason."

CHAPTER
EIGHT

"Did you..." Eva shook her head in amazement. "Did you wait in the dark this whole time to say that?"

Jack Pinchot gave Eva a sneer, his facial scar looking particularly gruesome in the green hue of the night-vision goggles.

Footfalls from the stairs filled their ears. Nash removed his goggles and motioned for Eva to do the same. He turned on the table lamp and yelled, "He's in here, boys."

The two slightly bemused figures of Bishop and Claude piled into the increasingly crowded study, removing their goggles as they did. Their guns at the ready, they turned to Nash with curious faces. Unfortunately, Nash couldn't sate their curiosity—he was as confused as they were.

Blinking several times to help his eyes adjust, with his gun still at Pinchot's head, Nash asked, "Who's the dead guy?"

Everyone but Nash and Pinchot tensed—the corpse in the kitchen was news to them.

With a nonchalant air, Pinchot replied, "A bad man who deserved his fate."

"And what fate was that?"

"To be tortured and strangled."

"Why?"

"Because he asked me nicely?"

"Nobody enjoys being strangled."

"I don't know, sometimes some consensual light choking can be fun." Seeing the stern faces surrounding her, Eva held up a defensive hand. "Not the time for a witty observation? Got it. Jeesh."

Nash pressed the gun against Pinchot's head. "Why did you strangle him in the kitchen?"

"Better than shooting him. Do you know how hard it is to get bloodstains out of travertine tiles?" When the statement didn't garner any more response than Eva's attempt at humour had, Pinchot went on. "Yousif had vital information I required. In the process of him providing said information, he came to the end of his violent and harmful existence. I for one will not lament his passing, and if you knew anything about the vile little dipshit you wouldn't either."

Pinchot appeared entirely unconcerned that four armed invaders had stormed into his safe house. In fact, he was altogether relaxed, perhaps artificially so. It seemed to Nash that he had expected them.

"What information were you after?"

"Would you believe me if I said his recipe for Hungarian Chicken Paprikash stew?"

"No, I wouldn't." Nash glanced at the others. "How long were you torturing him? No one has entered this place since the day before yesterday. You must have taken your time, he's only been dead for an hour."

Pinchot let out a theatrical sigh. "Do you want to judge or stop a terrorist attack?"

That gave Nash pause. Was he talking about the same terrorist attack Harry had found a reference to deep within the bowels of Tartarus? The one that would lead to Cavendish's lauded grand scheme. Was all this connected?

The expressions exchanged around the room echoed Nash's feelings. This wasn't going the way they'd expected.

Claude pulled out his phone and pressed a button. "Boss, you better get in here."

He hung up without another word being spoken. Sophia soon arrived and was brought up to speed. Once done, she and Nash spoke no words but silently exchanged a progression of looks and came to the same conclusion: Pinchot would not give up his secrets easily. She asked Claude to cover the entrance in case Pinchot was stalling for a rescue. Nash, Sophia, Eva and Bishop remained. Sophia rolled her hand, indicating Nash should take the lead.

"Who was Yousif?"

"Does it matter?" Pinchot settled into his chair, decidedly relaxed. "He's dead."

It was late and Nash was so out of sorts with time zones he didn't know if he was exhausted or wired. He may as well press his luck and lay it all on the table.

"We know Cavendish was sprouting his grand scheme as the salvation to Tartarus's fuck-ups." Nash scrutinised Pinchot's face and saw the reaction he'd hoped for. It was Pinchot who'd been the instigator of said fuck-ups. He wasn't nonchalant anymore. "And we know he's planning a terrorist attack under the absolutely subtle name of Ultimate Sacrifice." There was the slightest twitch in one of Pinchot's eyes—there was the tell Nash had been looking for, confirming the American was familiar with the operation. "The scheme is to fool an existing terrorist cell into believing their organisation is supplying the plan and means to carry it out. For them, everything would seem genuine; the bombs, the target, everything. I'm guessing your friend Yousif back there was part of the cell. What Yousif and his cohort didn't know, however, was that Tartarus will warn the legitimate spy agencies of the imminent attack. And when they are dismissed and the attack succeeds, Tartarus will claim the biggest I-told-you-so in history, putting them well on their way to being a respected and legitimate private spy organisation. Did I miss anything?"

Folding her arms and leaning against a bookshelf, Sophia's brow creased into an impressed frown.

"Not bad for an Englishman." Regaining his earlier arrogance, Pinchot released a sinister leer. Straightening his back, he inhaled deeply. "Most of it is accurate. You missed some important steps, but you have the idée générale."

Nash shot Sophia a glance. She hadn't been introduced, nor had she spoken. None of her team had, other than Claude's phone call to bring her in, and he'd done a reasonable job at a neutral accent. The sprinkling of French meant Pinchot was aware this was at least in part a DGSE operation.

"Why am I here, Pinchot?"

"Why are any of us here?" He waved his hands around with a shit-eating grin.

"This isn't a coincidence." Nash sat at the edge of the desk, his mind swimming through the thousands of possibilities until he saw the solid land of what he concluded was the most likely scenario. "You made it possible for us to find the information about Ultimate Sacrifice. We used your login, after all. Then you dropped clues so the DGSE could find me. You even provided them intelligence as to where *you* were. You stage-managed all of this. The next question is, why?"

There was another possibility Nash didn't verbalise. The individual in front of him was wily, canny and murderous, never someone to turn your back on. This whole situation could all be an elaborate trap.

Pinchot gave Nash an expression that was close to admiration. "I know this may come as a shock to you, but there are not many people in the world I can trust anymore."

"Diddums." It was the first time Eva had spoken in some time.

Pinchot's eyes narrowed. "But I do know a group of individuals who share my goals, though we don't share the same principles. I thought it prudent to rally them, and you, to assist in a task impossible for an individual, albeit a highly talented and intelligent one, to perform by himself."

"You want our help to stop a terrorist attack?"

"No." Pinchot leaned forward, his voice low. "I want your help to kill Cavendish."

Nash needed to walk around the block to quench his powerful impulses. Pinchot had an uncanny ability to draw out the worst in him. At every turn he'd been influenced by the man in some way. It was Pinchot who'd first embroiled Nash in this mess when he'd sent assassins after him at Devil's End. He'd tried to kill Nash multiple times and orchestrated Tartarus's worst crimes. But here he was holding all the cards, again. They hadn't been hunting Pinchot, he'd been hunting them. The master manipulator had struck again.

Nash needed more. He needed to know what lay beneath Pinchot's words. With him, there were always schemes within schemes. He returned to the study to extract more from the man who was the mirror opposite to Nash.

"You told me the next time we met you were going to kill me." Nash tried to sound as casual as possible, not the easiest of tasks when talking about your nemesis's death pact.

"Maybe the time after that." The subject seemed to amuse Pinchot. "I've still got a few years in me. Never say never."

"Why are you doing this?" Nash asked, feeling the others' eyes on him. "And before you say revenge, there has to be more to it. You could have escaped to a tropical island somewhere and lived out the rest of your life drinking cocktails and lying on the beach. You could have disappeared."

Nash was reminded that he'd tried to do exactly that with less than stellar results.

Pinchot shook his head vehemently. "I'm fucked no matter what I do." He waved his hands in the air. "Tartarus are after me and they'll never stop. Never. My own government's the same. Either way I'll be dead before the year's out. I've got nothing left. Except revenge." He savoured the word. "My final poetic act will be to take out the bastard who's been lying to me for years, manipulating everything from the shadows with me clapping along like the good dancing monkey I am, only to be stabbed in the back when he didn't need me anymore." As if as an afterthought, he added, "Oh, and for killing the board. Fuck Tartarus and fuck Ramsay Cavendish. That son of a bitch is going to die screaming for everything he's taken from me."

Nobody said anything for a moment, letting the anger subside. Nash wasn't one for revenge. He'd seen souls hollowed out chasing it. On his journey to becoming a better man, Nash had learned to let the pursuit of retribution fall by the wayside. It was never the answer, though it always pretended to be. Revenge wasn't the end of one's torment, only the harbinger of more. Pinchot had not learned that lesson, and for an instant Nash felt pity for him. It was fleeting.

"Cavendish is here in New York?" Sophia asked.

She'd let Nash lead the questioning. Multiple cross-examiners could be a useful tool when you wanted to discombobulate the target, but they needed Pinchot as lucid and focused as possible. He was irritated enough without numerous people interrogating him. Luckily Sophia had asked the question that was next on Nash's list.

"He is. I'm guessing he doesn't trust his underlings to carry out the attack without fucking it up. He made sure Tartarus hired the best in the world but here he is getting his manicured hands dirty. I know when and where he's going to poke his head out of the trenches and the precise moment you can stop the attack and I can get to him."

"Where's that?"

Pinchot swung his index finger from side to side: *not yet*.

He was playing them and Nash didn't like it. He folded his arms. They knew more than they had before, but they still weren't in control. Nash was sure they couldn't trust Pinchot, ever.

"Who's carrying out the attack?" Nash thought he could at least get that.

"Yemen terrorists. An offshoot of an offshoot an Iran-backed Hezbollah cell who think they'll raise awareness about the ongoing conflict between the righteous and just freedom fighters and the Republic of Yemen's evil government under the leadership of their idiot president. In reality they're working for Ramsay Cavendish, a man they've never heard of. They have no idea he's the one who's really guiding them to meet Allah at the gates of heaven. Poor ignorant bastards."

Nash took the information onboard and decided to change tack, bringing the focus a little closer to home for Pinchot.

"You know what happened to the board?"

Bishop asked the question, and Nash wished he hadn't. Pinchot was fired up enough as it was.

Pinchot clenched and unclenched his fists. "I should have seen it coming, but by the time I realised what the hell was happening it was all over. I'd worked with those people for years, many of them I called friends, and now they're dead because some sadistic megalomaniac didn't want the competition."

"Is that your theory?" Nash asked. "That's why Cavendish had them killed?"

Throwing up his palms, Pinchot asked, "What else is there?"

"There's a new regime and Cavendish is clearing the decks. Excising the remnants of the old guard." Nash chose not to mention that it had been under Pinchot's rule that Tartarus had perpetrated their most reckless and murderous acts, those that had caused Cavendish to step from the shadows in the first place. Everyone in the room knew it, but given the precarious state of the uneasy alliance, it seemed best left unsaid. "You seem to have escaped unscathed."

"Oh, they tried." Pinchot issued a sardonic sneer. "A hit squad tracked me down in Montpellier. They almost had the drop on me, but I managed to take two out before they retreated to lick their wounds. Got out of France the same day."

"The rest of the board didn't fare so well," Nash observed.

"The board Cavendish handpicked, me included. The board he manipulated from the very beginning. Is that the old guard you referred to?" Pinchot's words were bitter, coated in venom. "Every member of the board did that old man's bidding—we were loyal to a fault. He didn't have to kill them, they would have continued to follow; they all believed in what he was doing. The egotistical puppet master had all his little marionettes dancing for his amusement, right up until he decided to cut the strings." Pinchot's jaw set like concrete. "No, he removed them so there would be no one left to challenge the man who would be king."

"Except you?"

Pinchot's head slowly swivelled towards Nash. "Except me."

He was certainly bitter, perhaps even unhinged. Nash's concern only grew. Misgivings notwithstanding, they had a terrorist plot to stop.

While they couldn't afford to take Pinchot at his word, the evidence he presented was certainly compelling. In the space of an hour he demonstrated proof of the forthcoming terrorist attack. Tartarus had found and infiltrated a Yemen terrorist cell. In the past year their handlers—the real ones —had provided them several targets, set operations in motion, only for the plans to fall apart for various reasons. The cell were primed and ready to execute whatever order their leadership issued. Except, it wasn't their leadership giving the orders anymore.

Terrorist cells don't have access to their leaders. If they did, there would be too much potential for even the tiniest of breaches to bring the whole organisation tumbling down like a house of cards. Each cell was self-sufficient and capable, they just needed instructions. Tartarus was only too happy to provide them.

Every piece of evidence Pinchot provided from his clunky hard case laptop was scrutinised and challenged by Nash and his team. When they asked for proof, electronic trails, supporting evidence, Pinchot provided it every time. If it was a ruse, it was an exhaustive and convincing one. No question or request for verification went unanswered. No matter what they asked, Pinchot had not only the response, but the files on his laptop to back it up. And what emerged was a horrific and murderous plan.

The operation was to take place the following day, timed to ensure there would be the most civilians around. Tartarus had chosen their target well and the Yemen cell leapt to the assignment with relish, knowing the deaths would be catastrophic. Nash estimated a few hundred, possibly more. It had all been set in motion, and there was no one to stop the horrific event except for those standing in the room.

"Tartarus will send the vague warning to the CIA, FBI, Homeland Security and the rest this afternoon," Pinchot said, seemingly reading Nash's thoughts. "Their caution won't contain much in the way of elaborate detail, of course, but enough to garner attention. Twenty-four hours to give every major agency enough time to fuck themselves royally in the arse when the shit finally goes down."

Sophia asked, "What if one of those organisations takes Tartarus at their word and acts?"

"Then Yousif's mate's will probably die in a gun battle at their tiny little hovel instead of with explosives strapped to their chests." Pinchot shrugged indifferently. "Even if they are captured, there's nothing to tie them to Tartarus; they still think they're receiving legitimate orders from their Yemen masters. Tartarus will come out of this clean either way."

"Except what you've shown us." Bishop pointed to the chunky laptop. "We could take all this to the cops now. You convinced us, you'd do the same with them."

Nash was surprised the notion hadn't even occurred to him. He was so wrapped up in contingencies and counter plans he forgot the most basic thing. No normal human being would want death on an unimaginable scale. The cops, the FBI, Homeland Security and whoever else, when presented with Pinchot's files, would want to both prevent a horrendous fanatic assault *and* expose Tartarus. It was a long shot, but plausible. Salvation was within their grasp.

A malicious leer creased Pinchot's thin lips. Casually, he pressed a small indentation on the side of the laptop. A small black piece of plastic poked out and before anyone could stop him Pinchot gave it a tug. Within seconds white phosphorous smoke poured from beneath the keys. The whole laptop burst into a toxic billowing cloud of noxious gases, sending the team running from the confines of the study.

Coughing, Nash grasped Pinchot by the shoulders and shook him. "What the hell?"

"Magnesium strip," he hooted, indifferent to Nash's anger. His eyes fixed on Nash's. "That was the only copy."

"But you're condemning hundreds of blameless people

to die," Nash growled, shoving him against the wall in disgust. "We could have ended this here and now. We could arrest the terrorists before they harmed anyone." Nash let out a poisonous cough. "Why the hell would you do that?"

"It's quite simple: because I'm not interested in justice." Pinchot straightened his back. "I'm here for revenge." Seeing their gobsmacked faces, he continued. "I don't want to see Cavendish behind bars—not like that would ever happen anyway, but let's pretend there was the remotest possibility it could. So what? After everything he's done to me, the board, *my friends*, that human shit-stain deserves to die. Christ, even you know it, surely? With his power and influence he'll never even face a single charge. You saw how he manipulated past events and turned them back on you. I may be a master strategist, but that man is a god." He shook his head. "No, we play this my way and we all get what we want."

Sophia's lips pursed and her eyes narrowed. Nash had seen her make that face only a few times, and each time the recipient of the look soon regretted crossing her. He doubted Pinchot understood the danger he was in. The wrath of a full-flight Sophia Ocon was not something you ever wanted to trigger.

Slowly, she asked, "What is it you want, Mr Pinchot?"

He made a *fancy* face. "What I want, *Ms* Ocon, is for us both to win. You save the day and I destroy Tartarus from the head down by getting my revenge. Here's my one and only offer. You take me to the target tomorrow." He checked his watch. "Actually, today. You can stop the terrorists and I get Cavendish. Everyone wins."

"He'll be there?" Nash couldn't help himself interrupting.

"He will. You take me there and let me loose, I'll let you

idiots be heroes if that's what you really want. It's non-negotiable. I'm there or the deal's off. That's the only way this will play out. Do we have an accord?"

Looking at each of his companions, Nash saw the doubt dripping from their features. It was a reflection of his own uncertainty.

"We need to discuss this." Nash motioned around the room.

"Take your time." Pinchot clasped his hands in front of him. "I'm not going anywhere."

Nash, Eva, Bishop and Sophia moved to the kitchen, leaving Claude to guard their prisoner. Though from the smugness on Pinchot's face, it was uncertain if he believed he was a prisoner at all.

The mounting doubt was most palpable on Sophia's face. "What I don't understand is—"

"How giraffes throw up?" Eva asked.

"What?" Bemused, Sophia gave a slight shake of her head.

"Why paper beats rock?" Bishop suggested. "I mean, you're just wrapping a rock, it's still a fucking rock, so why does paper win? It doesn't make any sense."

"No... I—" She turned to Nash. "Do they always talk like this?"

"You get used to it." Nash rubbed his beard. "He's obviously a high-functioning sociopath. He cares nothing for others, seems utterly incapable of empathy and would sell any of us out if it got him what he wants. The question is, what do we do with him?"

"We can't afford to take him with us," Eva growled in a low voice. "He's a loose cannon. The way that twat's wound up, he'd sacrifice hundreds of lives just for the chance to shoot Ramsay Cavendish in the dick."

Sophia blinked at Eva's choice of words. "Quite."

If Nash was to hazard a guess, he'd say Sophia was more open to the idea of taking Pinchot along than Eva. He had to admit, their options were limited.

"I will add," Bishop's voice was an unusually measured timbre, "we now have no evidence, no intelligence, apart from what's stored in the dark recesses of that man's mind. He's not going to give it up freely. He's an intelligent man, he knows what leverage he possesses." Bishop inspected his immaculate fingernails in faux casualness. "We could torture it out of him."

Nash had flashbacks to when he'd done exactly that to Pinchot, and it wasn't a pleasant memory. The event haunted him still, a none-too-subtle reminder of how quickly he could slide into the brutal man he'd once been. Thankfully, Sophia spoke before he could.

"No torture. He's a US citizen on US soil. I don't intend on spending the rest of my career on trial for him. I don't think we have much choice."

The lack of counterarguments reinforced the inevitability of their situation. They exchanged looks, hoping someone would come up with an alternative. No one did. Bishop finally verbalised what they all knew but didn't want to acknowledge.

"I guess we're making a deal with the devil."

CHAPTER
NINE

"They certainly picked a visible target."

Sophia wasn't wrong. The Vessel, the land-mark attraction at NYC's Hudson Yards, was visually striking, as well as supplying a fantastic view of the city. It was comprised of one hundred and fifty intricately interconnecting flights of stairs. Some called it Manhattan's answer to the Eiffel Tower but Nash thought of it more as an M. C. Escher nightmare. It had been closed for a number of years due to a string of suicides, but it was open that day, for the first time since 2021, for a special once-off Presi-dents' Day holiday event. The morning was the first bright and sunny day after a long cold winter. Those factors combined guaranteed one thing: it was going to be excep-tionally busy. That equated to more victims.

No matter the threats, Pinchot wouldn't give up where the terrorists were holed up. That, of course, would be too simple. Pinchot had only one target and it wasn't Yemen terrorists.

The deal Nash and his team had struck with Pinchot was as simple as it was fraught with issues.

Pinchot had promised to reveal how to identify the terrorists in exchange for a chance to kill Cavendish. Nobody was sure if the deal would hold; on either side.

Due to Pinchot's mishandling of Tartarus's activities, Cavendish doubted his organisation's ability to correctly carry out any operation without his direct oversight. According to Pinchot, Cavendish would observe the attack from close by, calling the shots to ensure their unwavering allegiance. As his entire play for acceptance depended on a flawless execution of his coveted "grand scheme", it was no surprise that the one who'd manipulated Tartarus from day one would want to oversee it.

Pinchot insisted he wouldn't tell them how to find the terrorists until he'd sighted Cavendish. That meant letting at least part of the terrorist's plot play out, which made the situation increasingly dangerous. Nash's mounting dread only multiplied with every passing minute.

Pinchot swore Cavendish would observe the terrorists on their way to The Vessel as they made their way through the adjacent Hudson Yards shopping mall. The terrorists were due at ten, which was two hours away, so it was assumed Cavendish could make his appearance at any time. Sophia's team, minus one, were stationed around the entrances to the mall. Claude was riverside, keeping an eye on the main entrance, ready to alert the others via radio comms should Cavendish arrive. Alain did likewise, covering the delivery entrance on the street on 10th Avenue. Baptiste the not-waiter guarded their impromptu guest in a faux baker's van parked on West 34th Street, while Sophia, Eva, Bishop and Nash stood outside the van in an awkward silence.

Everyone was wired, tense and over-tired. They'd checked and double-checked comms and weapons and had gone over the variations of the plan countless times. There was nothing left to do but wait, and the inaction put them even more on edge.

The lack of preparation combined with the countless unknowns would make any espionage team nervous, but given the stakes, it was bordering on untenable, even for these seasoned agents. The stress was palpable on each of their faces. Nash forced himself to unclench his muscles. He needed to be loose and ready for what was to come, whatever that might be. Everything depended on it. He'd never felt more like a cigarette in his life.

"We should have tortured him," Bishop said, as casually as if he'd made a comment on the weather.

Sophia thrust her hands deeper into the pockets of her camel-hair coat. There was still a chill in the air. "I told you why it was a bad idea. Plus, we didn't have time. The best torturer in the world would need ten times longer than we had to get the information out of him."

"You've never seen me work. I can be quite motivating."

Sophia's lips curled into a smile until she saw that Bishop was deadly earnest. Nash's edginess got the better of him and he opened the rear of the van. Baptiste's gun flicked from Pinchot to Nash, and his gaze flicked to Sophia. When she gave the slightest of nods, Baptiste's gun swivelled back to Pinchot. Sophia joined Nash inside the van and shut the door behind them.

Pinchot's hands were cable tied to an anchor point on the floor of the van. Even with his hunched back he seemed casual, at least on the outside.

"How many?" Before the inevitable *how many what?*, Nash added, "Terrorists."

Pinchot gave a theatrical drop of his bottom lip.

"What's the matter? Can't keep up your end of the bargain?" He turned to Sophia. "Him not being able to keep it up must be so frustrating for you, no?"

Sophia was too much of a pro to show that the comment had any effect, though the moment Pinchot turned to Baptiste, her eyes darted to Nash. She was as concerned as he was. They were running out of time.

"How do we find them!" Nash screamed.

There was a knock from outside and Eva's muffled voice asked, "Is everything okay in there?"

Pinchot shook his head. "No Cavendish, no terrorist spotting intel. That's the deal."

Sophia leaned forward. "People are going to die!"

"Only one people I care about."

Nash clenched and unclenched his fists, and not at the bad grammar. "At least tell us how many there are so we can deploy the right number of teams."

Pinchot considered this for a few moments. "Three." There was a long pause. "I think."

"You *think*? What the hell?"

"The plan I saw catered for four—two for carrying and detonating the bombs, two as a backup in case anyone couldn't complete the mission for any particular reason. But the plan's a month old now. Things could have changed, and we have no way of knowing. So, four, minus one, if my arithmetic serves me correctly, equals three."

"Didn't you torture the information out of poor Yousif to confirm?"

"He was a certified terrorist, I don't think the moniker of 'poor' is particularly apt." The glare from Nash reminded Pinchot he'd neglected to answer the question. "He confirmed three, but that was at the end of our time together and he wasn't exactly what you'd categorise as lucid by then."

For all his meditation, for all his self-discovery and supposed enlightenment, Nash had an urgent and all-encompassing urge to leap over and beat the shit out of Pinchot until he told them what they needed to know. The surge of violence coursing through his veins gave his vision a red tinge. He wanted to scream with rage. If Sophia and Baptiste weren't there he was certain he'd have pummelled Pinchot, damn his pacifism to hell. Why would Pinchot hold back information that would save hundreds? Was he that far gone? Had hate consumed him that much?

Swallowing his mounting rage, Nash wondered just how different he and Pinchot really were. For all Nash's enlightenment, it only took the slightest nudge to bring out the persona a past MI6 colleague had nicknamed The War Machine.

Without knowing how to identify the terrorists their task appeared impossible. They had to search thousands of faces to try and ascertain which ones screamed *I'm doing something I shouldn't be*. As a spy, Nash had studied count-less profiles of terrorist attacks. He knew that before an attack, some perpetrators sweated profusely and practically screamed to be made, while others were as cool as an Arctic frost and gave away nothing. A sense of panic infused his bones. They were going to fail.

Another thought struck. It wasn't pleasant. Yousif's disappearance may have altered the terrorists' plan, meaning everything could be unpredictable. Even if Pinchot finally relented, his information might no longer be up-to-date, and perhaps wouldn't even matter. Nash felt the sweat on his palms.

With forced casualness, Pinchot asked, "When will you release me?"

Sophia replied, "When we've captured the *three* terrorists."

Pinchot's icy veneer was boiled away by his white hot anger. "That wasn't the agreement!" He would have strangled her if not for the ties and Baptiste's hand on his shoulder. "I tell you how to get them then you let me go. *That* was the deal."

"You haven't told us anything." Sophia's voice was higher, the pressure evident in her tone. "The deal was we'd let you go in exchange for how to find them. You've failed to provide that information, so..." She motioned to his restraints.

Pinchot struggled against those exact restraints. "I can't get to him from here. If I wait for you lot of incompetent idiots to grab them I'll miss my chance, or worse, you'll scare him off. Either way I lose my chance." Regaining his composure, he lowered his gaze. "I'll tell you how to find them but you have to let me go now! Free me and you'll know what I know."

Nash didn't entirely agree with Sophia's steadfast adherence to the agreement, but this was her operation and he had little choice. He may as well back her up.

He gave a slow, sad shake of his head. "We're trying to save lives here; you're after revenge. You're still sticking to the Tartarus manifesto of getting what you want and damn the human cost."

Pinchot gave a dismissive grunt. "And you're still putting your slanted outdated morals ahead of the greater good. Your pathetic pacifist manifesto is jeopardising everything."

Sophia folded her arms. "Can everyone stop saying manifesto?"

Pinchot ignored her. "My so-called vengeance serves your interests too, Nash. You let me cut off the head of the snake and you'll help stop Tartarus here and now, and you won't even get blood on your lily-white hands."

"There's a thing called justice."

Even to Nash's ears the statement sounded hollow. The sympathy in Sophia's eyes only compounded his unease.

Pinchot let forth a bitter cackle. "You tell it to every law enforcement agency in the world who's after you, let's see how your beloved justice looks then. Hmm? Wake the fuck up, you pathetic child, the *only* way this all ends is if you let me go right now."

Pinchot's eyes were manic. He was unconcerned that his thirst for vengeance was putting hundreds, if not thousands of lives at risk. He only cared for one.

Nash studied Sophia. They had discussed the topic at length. She wouldn't let the dangerous man before them loose. They'd lied in the hope of the truth being revealed, but by now it was obvious Pinchot wouldn't tell them how to find the terrorists. There was no point keeping it a secret any longer.

"You're not leaving this van, Mister Pinchot," Sophia observed throatily. "Not until this is all over, perhaps not even then, and given your conduct this morning I'm inclined towards the latter. Now, you either help us save innocent lives or you let your hatred condemn them all."

"I'll fucking kill you!"

Pinchot yanked his bound hands and Baptiste struggled to keep him down. When he realised he couldn't free himself, Pinchot kicked out at Sophia as he let out a bitter yelp. His cries became increasingly incensed as Baptiste held him down.

Nash had to get out of the van; he was suddenly overcome with claustrophobia. It wasn't Pinchot, although he certainly wasn't helping. Their gambit had failed. They were on their own and had to find the terrorists without aid. Nash opened the door and leapt out on unstable legs.

Eva stepped around the corner of the van. "That sounded like it went well."

Pinchot's muffled cries continued. Sophia's raised placating voice came through the van's walls, but there was no reduction in his manic screams.

Nash turned to his team. "We're on our own."

Bishop scanned the crowd, which was growing by the minute. "Marvellous," he said in a tone which suggested it was the exact opposite of marvellous.

After a couple of minutes Sophia stepped from the van and tucked a strand of hair behind her ear. She always did that when she was nervous. "Mason..."

"I know."

"I don't think—"

"I said I know." He dug the heels of his hands into his eyes until white spots danced wherever he looked. He needed sleep, but that would be impossible in the next few hours, possibly ever. "Can we...?"

Sophia shook her head. "I don't think so. Not without..."

"Yeah."

Eva squinted. "Can the rest of us join this telepathic conversation or is this just for ex-shaggers?"

Ignoring her, Nash said, "Sophia, you need to inform your team this just a got a whole lot harder." He turned to Bishop. "We're going to need the weapons and comms pack from the driver's compartment, please."

The well-dressed man gave a two-finger salute and disappeared around the front of the van. As he did, Sophia stepped away and held her comms device to her red lips, speaking in hushed French to her team.

Eva gave Nash a nudge with her elbow. "What's going on between you two? There's a weird vibe. Like a sexy tension, but not. Are you two..." Eva looped her index finger and thumb together and made the appropriate mime with the index finger on her opposite hand.

"No." Nash rolled his neck. "But that's part of it."

"I'm confused."

"You and me both."

Eva punched him in the arm. "Spill."

Nash consulted the bight clear sky before his gaze returned to Eva. "I have a daughter." Ignoring Eva's gaping mouth, he pointed to Sophia, whose back was turned. "We have a daughter."

"What—" Eva swallowed, "and I can't stress this enough—the fuck?"

"She only told me yesterday. I still haven't got my head around it."

"I'm not surprised. That's some of the heaviest shit to lay on a human." She scratched the back of her neck. "Especially right now."

"Yeah."

"Yeah."

They stood in silence for a time.

"We'll talk this through later, yeah?" On receiving an affirmative dip of his head, Eva added, "In the meantime I suppose we should, I don't know, stop a terrorist attack or something."

"It's not like we have anything better to do."

"Right?"

116

Eva gave him another punch in the arm, apparently because she didn't know what else to do.

Sophia returned and clearly sensed the change in their deportment, but chose to say nothing. When Bishop returned with the backpack, Sophia addressed them collectively.

"My team is ready, although they're not sure what for exactly." She eyed them each individually. "This is not a sanctioned operation by my government. Even if I had time to explain I doubt they'd authorise it, which is probably a blessing in disguise, no?" Her countenance took on a more serious quality. "You all shouldn't be here, officially or not. And I definitely shouldn't be arming you." She thumbed Bishop's backpack. "They're untraceable, but should anyone ask..."

"We got them from a vending machine," Eva stated. "Got it."

Sophia accepted the comment and, using their bodies to shield what they were doing, distributed comms gear and weapons. One radio, one earpiece, one Beretta, one spare mag each.

Bishop cocked his head and addressed Eva. "What are you humming? Is that The Supremes?"

"Yes," Eva declared merrily, "Love Child."

Sophia's eyes darted to Nash, but she remained silent as she zipped up the backpack.

All business, Sophia's voice was low. "We need to remain absolutely focused. Check-ins are every ten minutes, no exceptions. We can't fail, not now. Everything depends on it."

Eva swivelled her shoulders. "If we don't succeed, you could call it the daughter of all fuck-ups."

Sophia's eyes narrowed on Nash, who became intensely interested in the manhole cover at his feet.

Bishop shook his head slightly. "Who the hell would say that?"

"People," Eva said vaguely.

"Touched in the head people," Bishop grunted.

Sophia sighed and turned to Eva. "He told you, didn't he?"

"No," Eva said, as innocently as a crooked lawyer. "And how could you not tell Nash he had a daughter?"

Bishop baulked. "Nash has a daughter? Since when?"

"Ten years."

"And you're only telling me now?" Bishop looked lost.

In confusion, Eva shook her head. "Nash only just found out."

"You just told me you've known for ten years?" Bishop scratched the back of his neck. "Oh... hold up. I thought when you said ten years, you meant *you'd* known for ten years. Yes, saying it out loud it does... I see where I went wrong there."

Sophia gripped Nash's arm and led him away from the van, then lowered her voice. "Are you sure about your team, him in particular?"

"Absolutely. At first, I thought he was an arrogant cad, self-absorbed and one-dimensional. I didn't get the appeal."

"I can still hear you," Bishop declared loudly.

Nash continued. "But he has a way of sneaking up on you."

Sophia seemed unmoved. "I'll take your word for it."

Rejoining the others, Nash asked, "Where should we be stationed?"

Without hesitation, Eva said, "Where they'll most likely

strike. Meaning in and around the weakest parts of the structure, as that's where it's guaranteed to cause the most damage and lead to collapse. That's where I'll be."

Sophia's forehead crinkled. "That's too dangerous. We should station the teams further back in the hope of identifying them before they get to the structure."

"Hope's not good enough." Eva's jaw was set. "You station your teams where you want but I'm going where they're ultimately going to be in case you miss them." She held up a hand to stave off arguments. "What's the alternative? We sit back at a nice comfortable distance and watch this place explode? Are we going to tell ourselves for years after, oh well, at least we kind of tried? We're either doing this a hundred per cent or not at all, and I'm telling you right now I'm giving this fucking thing absolutely everything I've got. I can't even go home without my own government shooting me in the tits so I've got nothing to lose. Now, I'm going up those fucking stairs and no cunting son of an arse-licking son-of-a-bitch is going to stop me."

All four stared at her in silence for a time, Bishop and Nash with arms folded, Sophia clearly dismayed. Bishop was the first to break the silence.

"Not really something you can argue with, is it?"

"No, it's not." Nash turned to Sophia. "We're going to position ourselves in and around The Vessel. Please notify your team accordingly."

Sophia's features morphed into a mixture of surprise and admiration, though Nash would be reluctant to put a percentage on either. Skewing her mouth to the side, she hit her comms device and spoke to her team. Sophia told Alain and Claude to continue their mall entrance surveillance but the rest of them would now be searching The Vessel itself and the immediate surrounding area.

Baptiste would continue to guard Pinchot. Their mission was exclusively to identify and neutralise the terrorists.

In quick succession Alain, Claude and Baptiste confirmed their orders and their readiness to proceed. They were set. All they needed now was a target.

CHAPTER
TEN

The crowds grew by the minute. Whether it was the holiday or the reopening of the iconic landmark, Nash wasn't sure, but what he was certain of was his growing dread.

He and Sophia stood by the base of The Vessel, elevated on a set of steps to see over the heads of the ever-growing crowd. The attraction had opened to much fanfare and those with passes climbed the steps of the massive structure, more closely resembling ants than humans. The crowds were thick, both in the attraction itself and in the surrounding public space connected by the shopping mall.

Nash and Sophia scrutinised every face in the crowd. A headache was forging its way through the back of his skull — the strain was taking its toll. He refused to acknowledge it. He couldn't afford to.

It was only a half hour or so before the scheduled time of the attack and they had yet to see any sign of terrorists, or more accurately, to knowingly identify any terrorists. There was still a high probability the terrorists would blend in with the crowd and carry out their attacks, killing Nash,

Sophia, Eva, Bishop and countless others. Their focus was on every member of the crowd, looking for the tiniest tell —*anything*—which would give the extremists away and allow Nash and the team to take them down. The non-stop concentration was beginning to drain Nash's sleep-deprived brain. He stabbed his palms with his fingernails to stay focused.

"I can't believe you told them."

Sophia's eyes remained fixed on the crowd. Nash wasn't the only one who was having trouble concentrating.

The break in their self-imposed silence was jarring. Besides the regular ten-minute check-ins, they'd stood side by side for the better part of an hour in total focused quiet. Sophia's gaze was unchanged, totally fixed on examining every face, gesture and change in body language in the ever-increasing crowd.

Not taking his gaze from the milling throng of New Yorkers, Nash replied, "They're my friends. I didn't tell them so much as they figured it out."

"They figured you had a child by looking at your stupid beard?" She stopped and added, "Your beard isn't stupid, by the way, it's rather distinguished. Damn you men aging so gracefully."

Nash accepted the compliment with a bob of his head. "Eva figured something was up and I filled in the gaps." It was his time to pause. "And don't you dare chastise me about aging. You're more beautiful than I remember, and that's a hell of a thing, let me tell you."

She elbowed his ribs. "You old smoothy."

"Enough with the old, thank you very much."

Sophia let loose one of her legendary belly laughs, part amusement, part tension relief. Nash was conflicted. Here they were, searching for terrorists who had been deceived into perpetrating a hideous and violent act that would take hundreds of blameless lives. They had no plan, no way to identify them. The clock was ticking and the threat of a fiery death increased with every passing second, and yet he couldn't think of anywhere else in the world he'd rather be than there with Sophia.

"What's she like, Sabine?"

Sophia's smile remained in place, but it now held a shade of melancholy. "She's super smart, although her school results don't always reflect it. She a little too smart for her class. She devours books. She's currently ripping through the *Hitchhiker's Guide to the Galaxy* novels."

"They've always been some of my favourites."

"I know." Sophia's voice caught slightly. "That's why I gave them to her."

Too shocked to say anything for a moment, Nash worked to compose himself. "Does she know about me?"

"I've never lied to her. When she was ready, I told her the truth. She knows about you."

"Has she asked to meet me?" Nash realised he may have rushed the delivery of the question.

"She has." There was the slightest hint of hesitancy in her tone, unusual in the strong woman. "I told her one day we may organise a meeting if we're still all amenable."

"So you were intending to tell me one day?"

"One day," Sophia smirked, still scanning the crowd, "but nowhere near as clunkily as I actually did. C'est la vie."

About to ask more, Nash was distracted. High above the growing crowd a drone buzzed, stationary, adjacent to The Vessel. He watched it hover for several moments before Sophia quietly cleared her throat to regain his wandering attention.

Sophia said, "My father spends his weekends in a field

flying those things around with the silliest goggles you've ever seen. He's even teaching Sabine now."

"Yes," Nash replied, his attention still focused skyward, "that's the thing. In a field."

"I don't get it."

Nash pointed up. "You're not allowed to fly drones in a city, not without getting through a mountain of bureaucratic red tape. Especially not at an attraction where they're concerned about bad publicity from suicides. They wouldn't take the risk."

"So..."

"I'm guessing it's connected to the terrorists somehow. Surveillance, proof, gloating, whatever."

"And they only have limited battery power... so..."

They hit their comms buttons simultaneously. A renewed sense of urgency surged through them. Whatever was coming was mere minutes away. With a flurry of chatter, the group redoubled their efforts with a state of resolve Nash would have thought impossible mere minutes ago. Every face, every movement, every piece of body language was scrutinised for any hint of malfeasance.

The crowd was shoulder to shoulder now. The line for The Vessel snaked to the perimeter despite the event being ticketed with specific entry times. Those not in the line were enjoying the first sunny day, even with the still-present chill, and many were laden with shopping bags. Collectively, they were in good holiday spirits.

It was then that Nash saw him.

In the line waiting to get into The Vessel, almost every member of the crowd glanced up to observe the drone as it dipped low before ascending once again.

Everyone except one man.

His eyes were transfixed on only one thing, The Vessel.

Nash elbowed Sophia to get her attention as he hit talk on his comms device. "Eva, red puffer jacket, twelve o'clock."

"Yeah, I have the fucker. Shady as fuck." Nash heard rustling through his earpiece. "Accomplice three metres to his left, your right. She has to be a bad guy—she's *definitely* a bad guy. She's wearing a denim jacket over jeans. Only immoral douchecanoes wear double denim. With a puffer vest over the jacket. So many fashion crimes."

Damn, Nash had missed the other terrorist but now that Eva had pointed her out it was obvious. She possessed the same glassy-eyed furious intensity as her compatriot. Both were in their early twenties, the ideal age for the susceptible and expendable.

"That's the three," Nash muttered, more to himself than anyone. Realising the comment needed clarification, he added, "Pinchot said there were three—"he stopped himself from using the word terrorist, given the crowd was shoulder to shoulder with them, "—people left after Yousif, or at least he thought there were. If those two are our targets and there's one flying the drone..."

"You're better at maths than I am," Bishop replied in his ear. "How do we take them?"

That was exactly what was occupying Nash's thoughts. Their jackets were far bulkier than the weather required; it was highly likely they hid undesirables beneath. If he was to hazard a guess, Nash would put his money on suicide vests. The triggers could be anywhere—concealed in a pocket, on the device itself, detonated remotely; it was impossible to tell.

About to verbalise his thoughts, Claude cut in over comms.

"Riverside status check, no change," he advised.

"10th Avenue, no change," Alain chimed in.

Eva was one flight of stairs above Nash and Sophia, on the first deck of The Vessel. Bishop was on a higher platform, positioned on the third set of stairs. All checked in.

There were no further check-ins.

"Baptiste?" Sophia asked, pushing the earpiece further in. "Baptiste, report."

Eerie silence was the only reply.

Nash took his eyes off the targets long enough to see the anguish in Sophia's eyes. Baptiste had never failed to reply when asked for a status check, always reporting that Pinchot was secure. Except now.

"Baptiste? What's your—"

"I'm terribly sorry," a harsh voice interrupted, "Baptiste is unable to come to the phone right now. He's come down with a sudden case of lead poisoning."

Nash hit talk on his comms handset. "Pinchot, I don't know what the hell you think you're doing but—"

"I *always* know what I'm doing, Mason. Always. Did you really think Cavendish was going to be watching from close by? He'd never be that reckless."

"Then why?" Then Nash thought, *oh right.* "Me."

Pinchot gave the slightest of chuckles. "That's right, you. You're the bait that's going to get me to him. You're the one who's going to enable my revenge."

Sophia grasped Nash's arm, fear in her eyes. Nash had seen that look countless times on the faces of those responsible for the lives of the people under their command.

Taking his finger off the talk button, Nash spoke quietly, "Baptiste is dead."

"You don't know that. He could be bleeding out, he could be..." Sophia couldn't finish, already knowing the truth.

Nash had to think. There were too many rogue elements at play. Two likely terrorists in front of them, another flying the drone—but there could be more. Pinchot was now on the loose. Baptiste likely dead. Cavendish could be nearby, or on his way, but both those possibilities were from the mouth of a confessed liar.

Nash hit talk on the comms device. "Pinchot?"

"Yes dear?"

"Go fuck yourself."

Pinchot could have escaped, but he chose instead to taunt Nash. He had his own agenda and Nash didn't have time for his bullshit.

"No, wait Nash. I have instructions for yo—"

"Secondary channel, now." Nash swapped channels before Pinchot could infect him with any more distraction. He waited for everyone to switch to the pre-arranged frequency, cutting Pinchot out entirely. "Eva, Bishop and I will take out the two targets. Claude, converge on our position, we're going to need the backup." He turned to the worried Sophia. "Sophia, go check the van to see if you can save Baptiste. Alaine, back her up. No time for a debate, everyone go."

As Nash put away the handset, Sophia gently touched his arm. "Are you sure?"

Before he could answer the decision was made for them. The lead target in the red jacket stepped forward; Double Denim fell into lockstep behind.

Pushing Sophia softly in the direction of the van, he gave her a reassuring nod. *I've got this.* She returned the nod and broke into a run. Nash stepped forward and unzipped his jacket.

"Lots of civilians in close proximity, Nash," Bishop advised in his earpiece from the platform above.

He wasn't wrong. Old Nash would have given Red Jacket a bullet between the eyes and hoped to hell he could get a clean shot in the ensuing panic to take out Double Denim. It would certainly neutralise the threat. But for better or worse, Nash wasn't old Nash. He needed to find a less lethal solution to derive the same result—neutralise the threat but with zero casualties, on either side. The only trouble was, he had no idea how to achieve that.

The other wild card was that the two prime suspects may in fact not be terrorists at all. They acted like it, but that didn't necessarily translate to being actual terrorists. Their status was ambiguous, and if their instincts were wrong they may miss the real targets.

As the suspects stepped onto the base of The Vessel a security guard placed a meaty hand on Red Jacket's chest, demanding his ticket. In response, Red Jacket pushed backward. He and Double Denim both drew guns and shot the guard in the chest.

Perhaps their status as suspected terrorists wasn't ambiguous after all.

The result was pandemonium.

People screamed and ran in all directions. Even before the hapless guard hit the ground, the two terrorists sprinted up the stairs directly toward Nash. Bishop and Eva were yelling in his earpiece but he couldn't focus on them, he had more pressing concerns.

Reluctant to take a shot with the scrambling crowds crisscrossing his line of sight, Nash did the only thing he could think of. He ran towards the terrorists. Sprinting down the stairs, he dropped his shoulder and rammed into Double Denim like a linebacker. Nash grappled for the semi-automatic Beretta in her right hand as she went sprawling backwards.

All Nash could hear was Eva in his ear screaming, "What the fuck are you doing?"

She had a point.

As the woman reeled backwards down the stairs Nash's left hand removed the magazine From of the semi-auto and pushed the slide against his thigh to eject the live round. His right hand moved like lightning, grasping one side of the woman's denim jacket while she was in mid-air and giving it a yank. She twirled like a demented tango dancer, and relinquished her hold on the pistol as her jacket unbuttoned to reveal a succession of vertically placed sticks of explosive with what Nash guessed were bags of ball bearings strapped to the outside.

Landing on the back of her head, she bounced down a succession of stairs, finally coming to a halt, her eyes open and glazed. Out cold.

Ignoring Nash's actions, Red Jacket sprinted up a set of stairs to his right, fighting through the crowd, which surged downward in panic at the sound of the gunshots. Eva came down the set of stairs to the left. The terrorist held aloft a gun to keep his path upwards clear.

A series of wires snaked their way to the inside pocket of Double Denim's jacket. Nash carefully extracted a handmade switch made from a household light switch. Inhaling deeply, he gave the whole mechanism a yank, separating it from the explosives.

Eva leaned over his shoulder and asked, "How did you know it wouldn't set the whole thing off?"

"I didn't," Nash said coming to an uncomfortable realisation.

"Good. Just as long as this isn't a slapdash operation." She hit her comms device. "One down. Bishop, Red Jacket heading your way."

"I see him."

Confirming Double Denim was indeed still out, Nash searched her, finding no more weapons. Eva checked the security guard for a pulse and gave a grave shake of her head. They bounded up the stairs, following the route Red Jacket had forged through the crowd. Eva followed with Double Denim's suicide jacket in hand.

It wasn't easy going. The weapons fire had caused panic, and everyone on the immense structure was fighting to leave at the same time. The guns in their hands helped clear the way, as did Eva's shouts of, "Police! Move, you cunts!"

Nash's first question was, *Why hasn't he detonated his bomb?* Red Jacket had had ample time to explode his own vest but hadn't. When they reached the next landing Nash had his answer.

The man's jacket was wide open, the explosives strapped to his chest on display for all to see. Streams of panicked New Yorkers stampeded past the instigator of their terror, oblivious. He was fumbling with the wires, shoving them into the light switch, which had detached from the main device. It must have dislodged as he jostled his way up the stairs, and now he was frantically trying to reconnect them.

Inside The Vessel was a labyrinth of interconnected stairwells snaking their way ever higher. The streams of frightened civilians flooded past, more concerned with the possibility of an active shooter than a man with a vest.

Seeing Eva and Nash approaching, Red Jacket stepped back and yelled, "I'll detonate it! Stand back!"

Holding one palm up to appear less of a threat, the gun behind his back, Nash said, "You're being lied to." He raised his voice to be heard over the panicked crowd

130

streaming past. "You're not following orders from your cell leader. You're being used. What you're doing has nothing to do with Yemen independence. Your organisation won't claim this as a major victory because they know nothing about it. You're going to kill all these people for nothing."

The momentary pause didn't last long.

"*You're* the liar!"

Nash could see a fraction of doubt creeping in, but realised it wouldn't be enough. The man was a zealot. It would take a long time to convince him, and as Red Jacket fumbled with the wires Nash realised it was time he didn't have.

In a low voice, Eva said, "We can just shoot him."

"I'd rather not."

"I rather would," Eva replied matter-of-factly. "If it's the difference between him and everyone else."

To emphasise the point, she extracted her Desert Eagle, which only spooked Red Jacket all the more.

"Not helping."

The crowd had thinned, with only stragglers flooding past them. Red Jacket stripped a piece of wire with his teeth and was anxiously stabbing it into the switch, his shaking hands making the task all the more difficult. They were running out of time and options. The structure was almost cleared. Bishop was somewhere above, though Nash couldn't be sure where.

"I have a clear shot," Bishop's disembodied voice said in Nash's ear, as if reading his mind.

"I just had that same conversation with your partner," Nash replied as quietly as he could to avoid alarming Red Jacket any more than he had to. "We're avoiding it if we can."

"Fine." Bishop's voice suggested it was anything but. The sound of movement filled Nash's earpiece. "Get ready."

"For what?"

The answer came from the most unexpected place. Bishop, replete in his three-piece suit, leapt from the level above, aimed directly at Red Jacket. It seemed to happen in slow motion. Bishop's suit fluttering as he dropped like a stone, steely-eyed determination on his chiselled face.

His leather boots landing on the terrorist's shoulders, Bishop knocked him forward as he landed awkwardly with a strained grunt.

Wasting no time, Nash wrestled the suicide vest from the dazed Red Jacket, who sported a bleeding gash on his forehead. In seconds, he'd stripped him of his devastating device. The mass of wires he'd been so focused on were yanked from his disorientated hand. Groggily, Red Jacket looked at the vest and the detonating wires in Nash's hand and swiped at them, but was too far away to get anywhere near them. He'd lost, his false mission a failure.

Ignoring the groans emanating from Bishop, Nash raised his gun and yelled, "Stay where you are!"

Red Jacket did not stay where he was. In fact, he did the opposite of staying where he was. He leapt over the railing onto the landing below.

"I need a little help."

Bishop didn't need just a little help, he needed a lot. Both his legs were splayed at unnatural angles and he was wincing in pain. Eva darted to his side.

Nash was about to rush down the stairs to intercept Red Jacket but was intercepted himself. Six cops converged on his position, guns raised, shouting overlapping orders. It was then Nash realised he was holding a gun in one hand and a suicide vest full of explosives in the other. He gingerly placed both on the platform before him. Eva, who likewise held a gun and vest, did the same.

With hands raised, Nash asked, "Have you guys ever heard the phrase this isn't what it looks like?"

The raised service revolvers and grim, fearful faces told him they had, and they didn't particularly care for it.

Eva turned to Nash as she raised her hands. "May I suggest an apropos phrase at this juncture?"

"Please."

"Twatnuggets."

N ash and Eva were roughly manhandled through the crowd. Bishop was treated at the scene by paramedics for suspected broken legs. Despite his bravado and charm, he was obviously in a lot of pain. Eva literally had to be torn away from him by the arresting officers.

As Eva and Nash were bundled into separate squad cars on 11th Avenue, Nash caught sight of an anguished looking Pinchot in the crowd. He took the pained expression on Pinchot's face to mean he hadn't succeeded in luring Cavendish to his death. Whatever twisted plot he'd concocted had failed. Nash only hoped Sophia and the rest of her team had survived getting in the way of Pinchot's revenge.

When the police cars arrived at Midtown Precinct South, Nash was sped through processing under his fake credentials. After that, he was shoved into an interrogation room where he was interviewed by police of ever-increasing rank, to whom he told the same story over and over again. He was an innocent bystander and saw suspicious activity, so he intervened. The communication gear and untraceable gun in his possession did not exactly lend credibility to his story; nor did the fact that he'd been caught holding a suicide vest.

Providing a description of Red Jacket to a succession of increasingly disinterested police officers proved pointless. There was no evidence Double Denim had been found. Nash suspected she'd regained consciousness or been dragged away by Red Jacket before the site was secured. As far as the police were concerned, they had their perpetrators. Why take Nash at his word when he and Eva been found holding the bombs? Of course, terrorists would say anything once apprehended.

After a couple of intense hours being shouted at by New York cops who weren't particularly fond of terrorists, Nash was left alone in the interrogation room. He was handcuffed to a stark metal table at the centre of the equally stark room, which was all white except for a mirror on one wall. After the clatter and jostling of his initial interrogations, it was deathly quiet. Nash was without water or food, and was beginning to feel light-headed. He couldn't remember the last time he'd slept, or what country that had been in.

Nash stared at the one-way glass and gave an unimpressed frown. To whoever was on the other side of the mirror the sentiment was clear: *you expect this to intimidate me?*

He then heard slow, methodical footsteps outside the room. The door opened with a creak.

"We really must stop meeting like this."

Nash was busy creating diamonds by the pure energy of his clenched jaw, and having a hard time coming up with a witty retort. Or any reply at all.

"Seems you're forever destined to fall into my orbit, aren't you, Mason Nash?" The newcomer closed the door behind him. He was dressed in an expensive navy Springfield Stripe Huntsman suit from Savile Row. He strode about the interrogation room with his customary arrogance. "It's rather perplexing, given your level of ineptitude, how you've managed to elude me until now. You must be the luckiest son of a bitch to ever tarnish God's green earth."

Surprised the edge of the table didn't snap in his fists, Nash glared at Ramsay Cavendish. In some ways, Nash was thankful for the restraints. Without them, every cell in his body screamed to leap up and tear the man apart with his bare hands. Pacifism be damned. His counterpart clearly sensed as much, keeping his distance despite the sturdy restraints.

Realising the one-way mirror could be used to his advantage, Nash said, "I don't know how you managed to weasel your way in here, but your friends," he gave the glass a wave, "should know this is all your doing. We stopped your insane plan."

Cavendish let out a tiny chuckle. "Oh, no need to play to the cheap seats, my lad. There's no one on the other side and no cameras are active. I've seen to it. No, you and I are very much alone."

"You're going to pay for everything you've done." Receiving no response, Nash tried to calm his mounting anger. "You set up a terrorist attack to fuel your own rampant ego and lie to the world."

Cavendish splayed a hand on his chest and gave a pantomime shake of his head. "Not me, my boy. You seem to have this mixed up. I didn't orchestrate any of this." He reached into his jacket pocket and extracted a USB drive.

"You see, I have evidence right here that the perpetrator of today's unfortunate events wasn't myself or indeed anyone remotely connected to my organisation. It points towards a group of four misguided and misled individuals." He leaned over the table, alpha male seeping from his pores as liberally as his Clive Christian aftershave, then rocked back on his heels and rolled the USB between his fingers. "Although it's only part of the story, of course. The other half is being manufactured as we speak by a team of highly experienced forgers—sorry, I mean to say *researchers*—who will find out who misled this little band of terrorists. Do you know who that individual would be? I have a disdain for cliffhangers, so I'll tell you. None other than Mason Nash." He moved his hand to his chest once more to mime disbelief. "Shocking I know, but when the perpetrator was discovered literally holding the bombs in question..." He tutted. "When the police are presented with that information, they'd have to be insane to come to any other conclusion, no?"

Nash wished he'd hidden a lock pick on his person to release him from the handcuffs.

"Although it's a bit redundant now, unfortunately. I won't be able to use it. Your friend Harriet has done an impressive job of trying to win your freedom."

That surprised Nash, though he tried not to show it. "Who?"

"Subtle." Cavendish groaned. "Harriet Gorton, or as you call her, Harry. She quickly scoured all social media and whatnot and created a surprisingly clear narrative that you and your little band of do-gooder idiots should be viewed as the heroes, not the villains. There's Instagram footage of you taking the woman's suicide vest from her and then heroically bounding up the stairs, where they have you on closed-circuit vision—which she obtained illegally, of course—negotiating with the actual terrorist before Charles Bishop bravely or recklessly, I can't decide which, leapt *onto* the actual terrorist. She very quickly instigated a social media storm and suddenly thousands of accounts were crying that the noble heroes had been wrongly accused and whatnot. A small crowd even formed outside this very station chanting for your release. It's made this," he twirled the USB in his fingers before returning it to his pocket, "superfluous. Shame. It really was quite compelling."

"Seems I owe Harry a beer."

"After all that I'd say she's earned a vineyard."

"Fair."

"She's mighty resourceful, that friend of yours. She's managed to evade us for quite some time, not an insignificant effort given the experts we have on staff. I'd be inclined to make her a job offer if she wasn't so tangled up in your do-gooder crusade." Cavendish inspected his faultless fingernails. "Pity her efforts were all for nothing."

The faint glimmer of hope was already fading, given Cavendish's condescending tone.

"It was all a very noble attempt, of course," he offered, "but for one slight, and I mean really very minor, aspect." Cavendish's thin lips parted in delight. "You're all the most wanted spies on the planet. As soon as I walk through that door the authorities will be told as much. Frankly I'm astonished they haven't come to the conclusion themselves yet, but you know, the wheels of bureaucracy and all that."

"Why not before?" Nash asked.

"Excuse me?"

"Why didn't you tell them before you came in?"

"Because, my dear boy, it gives us a chance to have a chat, doesn't it? Right now, you're just a suspected terrorist, albeit on shaky ground, but as soon as they identify you as the perpetrator of so many other crimes across the globe, every major agency will want their pound of flesh and I won't get a look in."

"Your crimes, you mean?"

"*Pinchot's* crimes, let's not quibble."

Nash gave Cavendish a leer, which seemed to surprise him. "He's coming for you, you know."

"Who is?" Cavendish asked. "Pinchot? He's dead."

"Not the last time I saw him."

"When was that?"

"A few hours ago."

There was no hiding Cavendish's sudden unease. "They told me he was eliminated in France."

Nash rocked on the chair. "Seems your people lied to you, buddy. I wonder what else they're not telling you?"

It was obvious Cavendish was deeply troubled—was it because Pinchot was alive, or because members of his own organisation had deceived him? Either way, his unflappable persona had just been flapped. Nash was satisfied that even in his compromised position he could still ruffle Cavendish's well-groomed feathers.

The older man brushed non-existent lint from his lapel and appeared eager to move on to another subject. *Any* other subject. "I live in a different world to you..."

"If only that were true."

"...where we provide the modern intelligence community what they so desperately need: *intelligence*. And I mean that in every sense of the word."

"At a profit." Nash tried to cross his arms but the chains on the handcuffs only got him partway there.

"Ask the Soviets how living without that went."

Nash shook his head. "Spies aren't meant to make a

profit. It's not their function, no more than a park or a hospital bed or the Prime Minister's nose-hair trimmer should make a profit."

"Does the PM have a nose-hair trimmer? Well, I never." In an instant, Cavendish's face turned deadly serious, with an emphasis on the former. "You and your little band will end your pitiful crusade here and now. You'll give the location of your team, including my wayward son, here and now and I'll let them live—you too. I'm sick of fighting you, Mason. We shouldn't be on opposite sides."

"We're not fighting you," Nash said with the innocence of a used car salesman. "We just happen to always be in the wrong place at the wrong time. Take today, for example. I was at the mall buying a pair of cargo pants and wouldn't you know it, there was a terrorist right in front of me. Quite the coincidence, don't you think?"

Cavendish gave a tired sigh. "You're rather tiresome." He thumped a fist on the table, redness flaring in his face. "Tell me where they are!"

"Lilliput." Nash waited a beat, then shook his head. "No, they moved. Gotham City, or was it Metropolis?"

"Tell me the truth!"

"Okay, but you're not going to like it."

"Tell me!"

"Fine. Almost all the hands you've shaken have had a dick in them."

If Cavendish could have flipped the table he would have. Clenching his fists in fury, he paced the white room in a white-hot rage.

"You think you're playing with me, you pathetic cretin? All you're doing is wasting my time. I'm embarking on the most crucial undertaking of the twenty-first century and you're throwing pathetic juvenile taunts about."

"You are."

Managing to stem the tide of anger, Cavendish clenched his teeth before going on. "What is it you and your team are trying to achieve, Mason? Do you really want to expose every intelligence organisation in the world? How they utterly failed to halt our infiltration? Do you have any idea how that will decimate their reputation for the next century? Do you really want to wreak that much havoc, that much chaos? You claim to be protecting your MI6, *my* beloved MI6, but in reality you'll be gutting them. You'll be giving every self-righteous ignorant politician the ammunition they need to tear out the pitiful funding they have to beg for. They'll be fighting foreign interests, crazed nationalists and violent extremists with nothing more than three graduates, a ten-year-old laptop and a fucking paperclip. You're not saving them, you're condemning them to the grave."

Quiet for a moment, Nash said, "So, what you're asking, if I have this correct, is now that you've compromised every intelligence agency for your own purposes with a private business that has no oversight and is not beholden to any government, you want me to, what, just leave it? Don't worry about it? Let you carry out your own twisted agenda?"

"We are the good guys. We are here to do good."

"Said every bad guy ever." Nash stared up at the stained white ceiling, fluorescent lights and sprinkler heads. "Last time I checked, the good guys don't go around killing innocent people to cover their tracks or selling illicit drugs for a bit of extra cash."

Cavendish's thin lips grew even thinner. "We're here to bring stability to the world. Share intelligence to stop real world threats. Act where government can't. We'll guide the major intelligence agencies to build a better world by showing them how."

"But that's exactly my point. Tartarus's motivations are led by frail and susceptible humans. The very concept of a private spy agency is abhorrent for that very reason: human beings are imperfect and weak. Pinchot proved the point better than I possibly could have. Tartarus is only as good as its leadership and I have to say, Ramsay old boy, so far it's come up very short."

"We've learned from our mistakes. We won't let that happen again."

Nash grimaced, not buying what Cavendish was shovelling and wondering how even the shoveller could. "Let's face it. You're going to lose." Nash leaned forward. "And I'm going to do an MC Hammer dance when you go down."

"A what?"

"You know the MC Hammer dance?" In spite of the restraints, Nash did his best to perform the moves from "U Can't Touch This". Lack of applause aside, he thought he did a reasonable job of it.

Cavendish glared at him for several moments. Nash wasn't sure if it was because he had no more counterpoints or had finally realised he couldn't persuade Nash with words.

"Why are you here, Cavendish? It's not about gloating, is it? That would just be gauche," Nash snarled. "I'm sure you'll spin events to try to win your coveted legitimacy for Tartarus." Nash put on a deliberate whiny voice. "See, I told you there was going to be a nasty wasty terrorist attack. Now invite me to the big boys' table, pwease."

"Will you give up the location of my son and the rest of them?"

"I'd sooner let you shave my scrotum with Freddy

Krueger gloves." Nash rested for a moment before adding, "It's a no, in case that was unclear."

Unlike the news about Pinchot's not pushing up daisies, there was no reaction on Cavendish's face. The very definition of a poker face. It was then Nash understood why Cavendish was here. They were alone, no witnesses. The man was here to kill him. He'd get information if he could, but killing Nash was the real aim. It was the only explanation that made sense. If he was telling the truth about Harry's herculean effort to prove his innocence, logic dictated that the authorities would ask why Nash was *actually* there saving the day when he was supposedly a wanted fugitive. Cavendish couldn't have him sprouting the truth, as there was a chance someone would take him at his word. Even with all the resources at his disposal to bend the truth, there was a chance Cavendish would slip up and the real truth would out. Unconsciously, Nash glanced towards the door. Cavendish caught it.

"No one's coming, in case you still carried hope." Cavendish pulled up a chair and sat on it backwards like some cool kid from an '80s movie. "Let's discuss where you've been getting your intelligence. I must say, you've vexed us tremendously."

Cavendish wanted to know what Nash knew. He was playing with his food before the kill. Nash wasn't about to play along. In fact, he had no intention of following any rules whatsoever.

"Now, here's what's going to happen to your friends if you don't tell me—"

Cracking his neck, Nash stood, so suddenly that Cavendish pushed his chair back, clearly fearing an attack. As well he should, although not as he expected.

Manoeuvring his long handcuff chains to allow him to

pick up his chair, Nash flipped it in the air and caught the leg to give him slightly more purchase.

"What do you think you're going to do with that? There's no lions in here, boy."

Using every ounce of strength he possessed, Nash threw the chair, not at Cavendish, but vertically.

Building fire sprinkler systems are always "on", as they have constant water pressure in their pipes. A heat-sensitive alcohol-filled glass tube holds the spray valve closed until fire heats the stopper enough to break it. Or until someone is reckless enough to break it of their own accord. For example, by throwing a chair at it.

The impact made a satisfying crack. By the time the chair landed on the metal table, an ear-splitting siren sounded and the fire system kicked in.

Standing legs akimbo, Nash realised just how smug he must appear as the water sprayed down. With barely contained wrath, Cavendish stepped forward, taking a syringe from the inside pocket of his jacket. *So that's how he intended to do it.* Nash had no idea what it contained but assumed it wasn't anything fun and would lead to a fast but naturally appearing death.

Two police officers burst into the interrogation room and the utterly drenched Cavendish was forced to hide the syringe beneath his jacket. Within seconds they were equally soaked. The older woman unlocked Nash's handcuffs while the younger's hand hovered over her service revolver, covering her partner. All four sploshed into the dry hallway where they were met by two more stern but less damp officers.

A grey-bearded officer gave Cavendish a review from boot to bouffant then asked, "Are you his lawyer, sir?"

Without replying, Cavendish pivoted and squelched

away towards the lifts. However he'd managed to ensconce himself in the police station, that knowledge clearly didn't extend to everyone, hence the fast, if somewhat soggy, exit.

As Nash was led away, he called over his shoulder to the departing Cavendish, "Don't be a stranger. We simply must catch up soon. We have so much to settle."

As the lift doors closed, Cavendish lowered his gaze. "We shall end this once and for all, mark my words."

Nash had no doubt their next meeting would be their last. One way or another, this was all about to end.

TWELVE

N ash understood he'd only won a momentary reprieve.

Cavendish had failed to murder him, but it certainly wouldn't be the end of it. He'd never stop, never give in until one of them was six feet under. Nash hadn't come this far to give up now. But for all this to end, he had to escape police custody. Far easier said than done. Sitting in his stark white holding cell, Nash didn't see a whole mess of options available to him. The only saving grace was the realisation that Tartarus's tentacles hadn't infiltrated the NYPD, as far as he knew.

Nash had spent an hour in the white brick-walled cell after being given a set of bright orange Department of Corrections overalls, as his street clothes were soaking wet. He'd also been given a much-welcomed warm meal. He'd had no other interactions. Eva had been arrested along with him, so he had to assume she was somewhere in the building. Bishop may be too, but given the extent of his injuries, he had likely been taken to hospital. He hoped Sophia was safe and hadn't run into Pinchot on her return to the van.

Baptiste's radio silence almost certainly meant he'd been killed. Nash could only assume Claude and Alaine were safe. But given Nash knew nothing of what had happened after they'd stopped the terrorists, that was pure speculation.

His real question was what Cavendish was up to. No doubt he was doing his best to spin the events to his favour, and plotting Nash's demise. That was a lot of unknowns, and a whole lot of waiting and seeing. Nash wasn't comfortable simply sitting around waiting for his fate to unfold.

A rattle of keys jolted him from his malaise. A fresh-faced officer opened the heavy steel door and poked his head in. He had a kindly demeanour, and the bulges under his blue uniform indicated he spent a lot of time at the gym.

"Hey there. Thought you'd like to know the DA's decided to file charges. They'll be presented in front of a judge for an arraignment this afternoon. If you want to contact a lawyer, now's the time." He leaned further into the cell. "Me and a few of the boys think that's bunkum, having seen some of the socials from today. But I came here to tell you if you want to make a phone call, you'll need to do it before you get passed over to DOC."

"Did they arrest the two we took down? The guy in the red jacket and the woman wearing the denim jacket?"

The officer gave a sad shake of his head. "They got lost in the crowd, I'm afraid. There's an APB out for them, so you never know."

"What am I being charged with, exactly?"

"That's not for me to say."

"But you think it's bunkum?" Nash was doing his best to sound as friendly as possible. "You must know something?"

"Article 490 of New York's Penal Law," he said seriously. "Terrorism, basically. For some reason it sounds like the DA's really frothing to throw the book at you." He waited a moment before adding, "Sorry about that."

Nash gave him a forgiving wave of his hand. *Not your fault.* "I could do with the phone call, though."

"Of course." The officer stepped into the cell and thumbed behind him. "There's a pay phone down the end of the hall."

"There was a young woman arrested with me." Nash stood. "She's Australian, but don't hold that against her. Do you know where she's being held?"

"I don't know, I'm sorry."

"That's fine." Nash cracked his neck. "If it's any consolation, I'm really sorry about this."

"Sorry about wh—"

Nash's fist connected with the officer's jaw with a bone-crunching *crack*. The officer's eyes rolled back as he fell. Landing face down on the metal bunk, he didn't move. The big man was down for the count. Nash had to concede he was the world's worst pacifist.

Looking down at the unconscious officer, he imparted another, "Sorry."

Nash quickly undid the officer's shoes, then unbuckled his pants and slid them down his legs. He was halfway through shedding his DOC overalls when he heard the cell door creak open, followed by, "Ahem."

There was really no arguing his way out of this one. Nash straightened up and held his hands aloft. Hearing no instruction, he turned slowly towards the door and saw a beaming face. Eva's face.

Casting her gaze towards the face down, pants-less

officer on the bed, she raised an eyebrow. "Do you two need a bit of time to finish up?"

Nash leapt across the room and embraced her. She wore the same clothes she'd had on during their mission, jeans and a t-shirt, but now sported a smart business blazer. She gave the impression of an off-duty lawyer.

She returned the hug, then stepped back. "I don't know how comfortable I am with a no-pants hug."

Nash pushed himself away. "Oh shit, sorry!"

"Joking. It's fine. You want to get out of here?"

Pulling on the officer's pants, he replied, "Oh, hell yeah."

They rapidly exchanged recent experiences. Eva's incarceration had been similar to his—angry interviews, cell, meal, a lot of waiting. She'd heard about the social media storm from an inmate who was put in her cell.

"Where did you get the jacket?"

"It's Sophia's."

Nash stopped buttoning up the police shirt. "She's here?"

That meant she was safe.

Seeing Nash's reaction, Eva gave him a nudge with her shoulder. "You still love her, don't you?"

Nash gave what he hoped was a noncommittal shrug.

Eva spoke as Nash put the rest of the uniform on. "She came blustering in under the pretence of being my lawyer and threw a whole mess of jargon at everyone. Either she's up on New York laws or she's watched way too much *Law and Order*." She chuckled. "She had the place falling over themselves."

There was no stopping Sophia in full flight. The woman was a force of nature.

Eva continued. "She demanded to speak to her client,

claiming I was a representative of the Australian delegation for the United Nations and she was a UN lawyer, and unless she got five minutes with her client there would be hell to pay."

"And it worked?"

"It not only worked, she managed to get me alone in a room for a few minutes."

"Baptiste?"

"Dead."

"Damn." Nash shook his head. "I saw Pinchot in the crowd. He obviously didn't get his revenge on Cavendish—the big man paid me a visit."

"Oh, shit. How did that go?"

"I'll fill you in later, but first things first, how did you go from the chat with Sophia to roaming the police halls in her jacket?"

She gave a wry smile. "The woman's good. She got them so knotted up thinking they were creating some kind of international incident, plus the whole shitstorm Harry created on social media, it was a confusing mess. Everyone's superior kept showing up, and the person in charge changed by the minute. She managed to bundle me into the ladies. I came out with slicked-back hair in a ponytail, her lawyer's jacket and a visitor's pass. I walked straight past the bickering cops." She glanced at the hallway. "We don't have much time before they realise what's going on. We need to go."

Given the gym junkie physique of the unconscious officer, the uniform swam on Nash. He did his best to tuck it in where he could.

Eva led the way out of the cell. "As far as I can tell there's, like, fifteen locked doors between us and the outside. No way we can bluff our way through all of them."

"You're saying we need a distraction?"

"I'm saying we need a giant fucking distraction."

"Let's see how much we can fuck shit up then, shall we?"

Eva turned, amused. "I really think I'm having a negative effect on you, Nash."

They walked with pace, but not enough to arouse suspicion. Seeing a door marked "Break room", Nash took Eva by the elbow and pointed her towards it. Despite her confusion, she followed.

Thankfully the room was empty. There wasn't much to it. A well-used dart board, a ping pong table, a coffee station and a fridge. Eva's confusion didn't dissipate.

Nash pointed her towards the fridge. "Is there any food in there covered in foil?"

He strode straight to the ping pong table, picked up several balls and grabbed a dart from the board. He then went to the coffee station and ripped open a tin of sugar.

Closing the fridge, she held two containers. "Someone's sandwich," she sniffed it and recoiled, "week old tuna by the smell of it and," she held it at arm's length, "something I don't even want to guess at, but it's gross."

She took stock of what Nash had gathered and grinned widely. "Oh, hell yeah! That's what I call fucking shit up."

The device would be as crude as it would be effective. Nash used the dart to stab a hole in each ping pong ball. Fashioning the foil into a funnel, he poured in the sugar. Once complete, he placed the dart at the centre of the balls, covering the whole thing in foil.

Removing the dart to create a chimney, he said, "I'm going to need a lighter."

Already ahead of him, Eva handed him a lighter she'd pilfered from the drawers. "Next to some birthday candles."

A wicked smirk crept across her lips. "And a few cans of Axe body spray."

"Oh, better."

Placing the foil ball on a tripod of aerosols, Nash lit the candles he'd bundled together with Eva's hair tie, creating a festive little fire. The flames charred the deodorant cans and the foil above it. Thick black smoke billowed from the funnel in an ever-increasing toxic cloud. Their impromptu smoke bomb working even better than they'd hoped, the two sprinted from the room.

The ensuing few minutes were nothing short of pandemonium. Smoke alarms screeched. The flammable cans exploded, likely resulting in a real fire and sending smoke pouring into the hallway. Overlapping shouts pierced the mounting din as panicked police raced in all directions.

In his ill-fitting police unform, Nash grabbed Eva and pushed her towards the nearest exit. A flummoxed grey-haired officer with her hand on her service revolver saw them approaching and buzzed them through the barred doorway with an officious scowl.

When they emerged on the other side Nash realised they were in the carpool. A mixture of civilian cars and black and whites were neatly parked at a forty-five-degree angle. In the far corner, a startled young officer was stationed next to a desk and a board full of hooks containing car keys. Daylight could be seen down the ramp to the street.

As Nash approached, the young man stood rigidly at attention. He gulped before he spoke. "Do you know what's going on? Is this another drill?"

The man's badge advised his name was Clements. His rank indicated he couldn't have been long out of the academy.

Nash used his best gruff voice. "I'm relieving you. You're to report to Johnson on three ASAP."

"Who, sir?" His voice practically broke. He gave Eva a sideways glance but said nothing further.

"Are you deliberately trying to kill your career, Probationary Officer Clements?"

The kid's eyes went wide. "No sir."

"Well, get to it!"

The kid practically sprinted towards the door they'd just come through.

"Wanna steal a cop car?" Eva asked in a low voice, watching the door close behind the startled officer.

"I think we've broken enough laws for one day. How about we just walk out of here?"

Looking forlornly at the rack of keys, Eva mumbled, "Well, this is some weapons-grade bullshit."

They strode fast down the ramp and were on the street and blocks away in no time. Finally exhaling, they ducked into a side alley and crouched behind a dumpster to gather their thoughts. There were plenty of those.

IT WAS WELL past nine pm by the time they reached Sophia's safe house. When Claude opened the door his face lit up, and the beefy man engulfed them in a bear hug like he was greeting his long-lost family. He ushered them in and led them to the back room where they'd planned the raid on Pinchot's townhouse. To Nash it felt like weeks ago.

Sophia sat on the corner of the table drinking from a water bottle. Bishop was beside her, in a wheelchair, both legs encased in plaster. Neither had seen them come in.

Pushing past Nash, Eva raced to Bishop's side. He

jumped in surprise and they hugged and kissed frantically, both talking over the top of each other. The emotional reunion reinforced Nash's understanding of how much the two were in love.

Sophia dropped her water and raced into Nash's arms. She squeezed him tight and he felt her back hitch as she suppressed tears.

"I'm sorry about Baptiste."

Composing herself, Sophia held Nash tight and spoke over his shoulder. "I am too. I worked with his mother long ago. This will wreck her."

It didn't make Nash feel any better. They all sat and brought each other up to speed. Alain was staking out Pinchot's place; everyone doubted he'd be stupid enough to go back there, but if there was the slightest chance, they were going to take it.

Bishop had fractured both his fibular and tibia in both legs. He'd make a full recovery, although the doctor who'd set his legs had warned he may require some physical therapy once the casts came off.

Eva cradled his face. "Thank you for being a stupid idiot and saving us. I'm so sorry about your legs."

"It's okay. I'm on so many drugs right now."

"You going to share or what?"

Sophia watched the two of them canoodle. "It was a most heroic act, jumping two storeys. They're calling him The Leaping Man on social media."

"Not the most original name," Nash observed.

"He did it for her. I get the impression he'd do anything to keep her safe." Sophia placed her hand on Nash's arm and spoke quietly. "I see it now."

"Sorry?"

"You told me Bishop had a way of sneaking up on you,

that he's more than he appears on the outside." She jerked her head in his direction. "I see it now."

Acknowledging her observation, Nash took a moment to appreciate the fact that they'd managed to narrowly escape Tartarus once again. They had been lucky, but that luck couldn't hold for much longer. This cat and mouse game could only last so long, and Nash was tired of being the mouse.

He realised for the first time how angry he was. Perhaps he'd been angry for far longer than he'd like to admit. He and his little group were always running, always on the back foot. They were meant to be the good guys, they shouldn't be cowering, waiting for the next blow. They needed to be on the front foot.

Nash stretched his arms above his head and addressed the room. "I have a plan for how to end this." He made sure he had everyone's attention. "Once and for all."

That surprised everyone; Nash included. He'd been mulling over the subject from the moment he entered the police cell. His thoughts had churned and fermented, but until that very moment he'd thought he still needed more time. Apparently not.

"What are you thinking?" Sophia asked, her forehead wrinkling at his sudden change in mood.

Nash clapped his hands together. "Has anyone seen *Blazing Saddles*?"

THIRTEEN

"You lived here?" Sophia asked.

The car threaded through the bright green countryside. It had been a wet winter and the fields were lush and full. Nash realised how much he'd missed it.

"For a time," he replied.

The pair drove the rental car along the country roads, enjoying the quiet after days of strenuous travel from the US to UK. Given their collective status, commercial flights were out of the question, especially since they'd never officially entered the United States in the first place. Bishop had used some nefarious contacts—"good" drug dealers who owed him favours—to smuggle them in a succession of small planes through so-called abandoned airports. It had taken four days, and they were all exhausted.

Eva and Bishop followed behind them in another rental. Alain and Claude were back in New York dealing with Baptiste's death. Sophia had taken a leave of absence under the pretence of working through her grief at the loss of someone under her command, although the truth wasn't too far from the lie.

The travel time had enabled Nash to help her through her grief, but also given them time to get reacquainted. Sophia was every bit as captivating and enchanting as his rose-coloured glasses remembered. The travel was laborious and tiresome, the company the exact opposite.

Sophia gripped Nash's arm as they rounded a corner and saw the village in all its glory.

"Oh my, it's lovely."

The clouds parted, bathing the sleepy Cotswold village and surrounding rolling green countryside in crisp morning sunshine. The few picture-postcard streets were lined with stone cottages in the shadow of the imposing Benedictine Abbey—St. Stephen's—on the hill above. Unsurprisingly, the village had been used for various TV productions whenever a quintessentially English country town was called for.

"You must have loved it here."

"I really did." Nash thought back to the last time he'd been home. "Until I didn't."

Devil's End appeared familiar yet completely foreign at the same time. He'd once thought he'd see out the rest of his life in the village. Given his plan, it now seemed more likely than ever that he'd do exactly that, but in a much quicker timeframe.

Not so long ago Nash had been a semi-happy schoolteacher, settling in with the locals, his violent past behind him—or so he thought. He'd fooled himself that this idyllic little slice of the country was where he could forget his sins. Unfortunately, those sins came looking for him.

He remembered his last night in Devil's End. He'd been doing some light flirting with a local barmaid, Lila, when assassins burst in and attempted to kill him. He'd dispensed them with reluctant violence, but in doing so had triggered a series of events he could never have foretold. He still recalled the look on Lila's face in the aftermath of the attack; a mixture of abject fear and horror. She was unaccustomed to such brutality, such bloodshed, yet Nash was surprised how naturally it had all come back to him. His old ways weren't anywhere near as old as he'd fooled himself into believing.

Nash parked, and in the car behind them, Eva followed his lead. They'd already set events in motion, but today they would implement the bulk of the plan in earnest. The rest of the team would arrive within the hour. The final stand would be made here.

Devil's End was the place where Nash had started his fight against Tartarus. It seemed fitting this was where he'd finish it.

The plan was as simple as it was thin.

Cavendish was scheduled to meet with MI6 two days from now, where he would capitalise on Tartarus's supposed brilliance at uncovering a terrorist attack ahead of time using their bleeding-edge intelligence gathering capabilities, unencumbered by centuries-old red tape and curmudgeon-filled bureaucracies. Although it hadn't been the shining success the former director of MI6 would have hoped—Nash and his team had seen to that—Nash had to concede Cavendish could be persuasive. It was entirely possible he could still put a positive spin on events, despite their best efforts.

But their best efforts weren't done yet.

Cavendish would know his greatest threat was still Nash and his team. They knew the truth, and could expose him and Tartarus on the world stage. They were the fly in the ointment, the wrench in the gears, the floating shit in the swimming pool.

Not a man to permit loose ends, Cavendish would do

whatever he could to stop Nash from ever posing a threat to the organisation he'd spent a lifetime dreaming of. Nash was counting on it. In fact, the plan hinged on it.

He turned the engine off and took a moment to take in his old house. The sight of the simple "chocolate box" thatched roof cottage gave him a warm glow inside. It was fleeting. What he'd thought would be his retirement house was to be the planning centre for his final battle.

Exiting the car, he and Sophia extracted their meagre luggage and Nash went to help Bishop out of the other car. His two plastered legs must have been uncomfortable, but he hadn't complained once. Nash handed him the crutches from the boot; Bishop took them with a thankful thumbs-up and followed the rest into the cottage.

The house was musty and needed a decent airing. Throwing the bags on the lounge room floor, Nash realised the place would soon be overcrowded. On the journey from the US he'd been focused on their tactics, and hadn't really thought about sleeping arrangements. Add it to the ever-mounting to-do list.

"This is how the modern bachelor lives, is it?" Sophia took in the surrounds. Eva and Bishop soon joined her.

"I'd hardly call it modern."

"Neither would I." Sophia gave a playful wrinkle of her nose. "Which one is mine?"

"Last door on the left."

She accepted the information then raised a well-crafted eyebrow. "This place could really use a woman's touch."

Nash pointed the way and Sophia sauntered past—the woman could certainly saunter. Once she'd disappeared around the corner, Nash received a slap on the arm from Eva.

"Ow. What was that for?"

"Dude, that was totally a hint."

He shook his head vacantly. "A hint for what?"

Eva glared at him. "You really are dense sometimes, aren't you?"

"Am I?"

Bishop dropped his crutches to the side as he flopped into the genuine Eames reading chair. "Yes, you really are."

There was a knock at the door and Nash opened it to reveal a tall lanky man and a much shorter Irish firebrand.

"Is this a town or a tin you keep your sewing kit in?"

Nash gave Paul and Nancy a hug. "Good to see you too, Nancy."

He motioned them in. It seemed eons since he'd been in Paul's company. But apart from the brief sojourn in Nepal, the whole Tartarus entanglement had started mere weeks before, though it felt a lifetime ago. He recalled that the first person he'd reached out to had been Paul, who hadn't hesitated to help his friend. Though at the time, neither knew the harbinger of their torment was Paul's own father. That was a conversation to be had over a very expensive whiskey later. For now, everyone needed to settle in.

Momentarily alone with Paul, Nash asked in a low voice, "Is it a good idea to have Nancy here?"

Paul slapped his friend on the back. "In our time as friends you unfortunately didn't have much of an opportunity to get to know Nancy, but there's one burning truth you need to know about my beloved wife. When her mind is set, there is not a force in the universe able to hold her back."

Nash returned the back slap. "I see why you married her."

Paul's head twitched in agreement. "So do I."

Screams could be heard from the lounge as Eva and

Nancy embraced as only best friends could. Sophia soon joined them and introductions were made. Paul and Eva went to work making sandwiches for everyone with supplies picked up on the way. The way the two quickly dropped into friendly banter and teasing reminded Nash they had been friends for many years, long before Eva became a spy. These people all had intricate ties binding them together. Nash would do everything in his power to keep them all safe. He had to.

A loud thump on the front door made Nash smile. Of course she wouldn't knock the same as everyone else. Opening the door, Nash was greeted with an aging punk rocker who looked to have fared better than the rest of them in recent times. Harry may have had a gruff exterior, but she pulled Nash into a fearsome hug and gave a relieved sigh. She didn't seem to want to let go.

Besides Sophia and Paul, Harry was one of Nash's oldest friends. She, along with Nancy, were the ones Nash most regretted becoming embroiled in these circumstances. Neither woman was a spy. Neither had been trained to deal with the ever-present threats hanging over their heads. Harry was a formidable private detective but, generally speaking, her clients didn't have teams of armed assassins and tended not to leverage every espionage agency in the world to haul you off to prison for treason.

Harry made her way inside and greetings were exchanged. She hadn't met Nancy, Paul, Sophia or Bishop in the flesh. She held the latter's hand a little longer than the others.

"Fuck me, the Swedes can be boring twats," Harry observed, dropping her backpack on the floor. "Lovely people, but they wouldn't know a good time if it sat on their face, and god knows I tried."

"To have a good time or to sit on their face?" Eva asked.

"Yes." Harry pursed her lips and turned to Nash. "Where's the booze at?"

"It's ten am?"

"Your question didn't answer my question."

Paul and Eva dropped a mound of sandwiches on the kitchen table and the group tucked in. It warmed Nash's heart to see them all engaged in friendly chatter and cama-raderie. It was amazing how everyone meshed so seamlessly together, as if they'd known each other for years.

"So, what's this end game plan of yours?" Harry asked between bites of an egg and lettuce sandwich.

Holding a cheese and pickle aloft, Nash replied, "Not yet."

"The gang's all here though, aren't we?" Harry looked around quizzically.

"Not quite."

There was a rap at the back door. With a chuckle, Nash half suspected the knocker had waited until that exact moment to knock. He always had impeccable timing. Opening the old door revealed a bald, grey-bearded man with arms the size of tree trunks. Nash always joked he was a cross between a lumberjack and a badass Santa.

Sebastian Hawk was the school principal who'd given Nash the teaching job at the local school, the reason he'd moved to Devil's End in the first place. Hawk had been Nash's SAS instructor back in the day and the two had been friends ever since. He'd been on sabbatical in Spain when Nash was attacked by Tartarus's assassins, and Nash had disappeared by the time Hawk returned.

Nash had borrowed a drug dealer's scrambler satellite phone in transit to the UK to call Hawk and ask for his old friend's assistance. The cost of the call was Nash's vintage Rolex, but he considered it a bargain. Once Hawk heard what Nash had been through, the challenges he faced and a broad outline of what he had in mind, the Scotsman was not only in, he'd already started to make a list of the gear they'd need. His old friend had offered to put his life on the line for the man who'd once done the same for him, no questions asked. Except to check how many guns Nash needed.

Introductions were made all over again. Hawk had a way of ingratiating himself with people quickly. His green eyes would hold someone's gaze and he'd ask them questions in his relaxed Scottish brogue, rapidly building rapport. Within no time at all they intermingled like old friends. It was remarkable to watch.

Over their early lunch the group traded stories, mostly about Nash, and filled his old house with laughter. He had to admit that was something that had been lacking even before Tartarus arrived. The place was filled with light once more.

The table was cleared and dishes washed, then they congregated in the now crowded lounge room. Ignoring the hour, Hawk helped himself to Nash's liquor cabinet and dispensed the most expensive whiskey, which was fitting as he'd been the one to buy it. He also handed out Nash's cigars.

Hawk told a tale about how Nash had gotten his foot wedged in a barbed-wire obstacle in a particularly brutal SAS course, much to the amusement of the rest of the group. When he'd finished, Nash spoke up.

"You're missing the last part of the story."

"Am I?" Hawk asked, his tone making it clear he knew perfectly well he had.

"Yes, you are. The next month I did it again and broke the course record."

Hawk lit his cigar with his silver lighter. "That so?"

"You know I did, you old bastard."

The two men laughed and clinked glasses, and a lull fell over the group. Now was the time to lay everything out. Sophia, Eva and Bishop had heard his plan, at least parts of it, on the long trip to the UK. For the rest, it was new. Nash took half an hour to let them all know what he had in mind.

The silence that followed was hard to put a name to. Nash hoped it was awe, but had to admit it was more likely stunned, or perhaps even dumbfounded. It was a lot to take in.

Hawk leaned back and took a drag of his cigar. "Nash, I always suspected you were a crazy son of a bitch but never in my wildest or drunkest imaginings did I suspect you were *this* crazy." He leaned forward, placing his elbows on his knees, and in his best Scottish accent said, "I'm fucken' in."

THE HANGMAN'S Inn was a four-hundred-year-old pub in the centre of the village. It was an intimate setting, with a smattering of tables and booths under a low ceiling with the bar taking up one entire wall. Deep chocolate wood, it was decorated with exotic bottles and knick-knacks accumulated over the pub's long history. Nash had forgotten how much he'd loved this quaint little slice of Devil's End.

Once everyone had gotten to know each other and planning had begun in earnest, Nash needed a break. More importantly, he needed to talk to Paul. The two were alone in a corner of the pub. It was late afternoon, not exactly peak time, which suited both men as they sat nursing their pints.

It had been an hour since Nash had sent the email. It contained only a few lines, but no doubt would have large ramifications for all. He'd sent Paul's father an unencrypted email stating that he was withdrawing from their fight. In an unemotional missive, Nash explained that New York had shown him what he was up against and he couldn't do it anymore. In no uncertain terms, he conceded to Ramsay Cavendish. All Nash wanted to do was retire to Devil's End, and he asked Cavendish to respect his wishes. The IP address would confirm where the email had been sent from.

It was bait, of course. There was no way the architect of the greatest deception of the twenty-first century would simply allow his nemesis to wander off into the sunset. He couldn't allow Nash to live, knowing the information he possessed.

While the two sat drinking, there was no doubt Paul's father was busy planning to exact his revenge for all the pain and suffering Nash had caused him. The entire plan counted on it.

Sitting with his friend, Nash found it was impossible say the next comment casually, so he didn't even try. "I spoke to your father in New York."

Paul bobbed his head. "That's funny, last time I checked I no longer had a father."

The silence was only magnified by the empty pub. Denise, the publican, was the only other person in the pub. She stood at the end of the bar drying glasses.

"Has he changed?" Receiving no answer, Paul added, "Did he ask after me?"

"No, he didn't."

"Then he hasn't changed."

Nash could only imagine what torment his friend had gone through in recent weeks. Having an estranged father was one thing, but having an estranged father who had created his own private army, infiltrated espionage organisations across the globe and orchestrated the murders of hundreds was quite another.

Nash swished the remainder of his beer around the bottom of his pint glass. "Given what's about to happen, how are you going to feel if we get ourselves into a him or us situation?"

"Mason, my friend," Paul looked Nash in the eye, ensuring he had his full attention, "I think we've been there for some time now. Will I relish it? No, of course I won't. But what we're trying to achieve here is far too important for my personal feelings to matter."

"They do matter." Nash placed his hand over Paul's.

"Thank you, I appreciate it, I really do." Paul gave a close approximation of a genuine smile. "But the fact remains, we have to end this. He's one of the most dangerous men on the planet right now. We can't let him win. Under any circumstances." He shook his head, then finished his pint. "We make our stand here. History has shown time and time again that power should never rest in the hands of any one individual. No matter what my connection to Ramsay Cavendish is, he must be stopped, and that's exactly what we'll do." He slammed his empty glass down like a violent full stop. "Another?"

"Please."

Watching Paul order another round, Nash understood it wasn't as black and white as his friend was trying to make out. Family never was, especially not Paul's. Regardless of his friend's consummate professionalism and unflappability, the coming battle was going to be difficult for him. Nash would do his best to protect his friend from coming into orbit of his father, but given the unpredictability of their plan, nothing could be guaranteed.

As Paul chatted amiably with Denise at the bar, someone else entered. Somewhere in her thirties, Lila Pickford was exactly as Nash remembered, wide-eyed and full of energy. She greeted Denise warmly and placed her bag and coat behind the bar, readying herself for the evening shift at the pub. Nash had only spoken to her once properly, and the two had semi-flirted, but then he'd been attacked soon after. Nothing quells a budding romance like gunplay and death.

Lila froze mid-sentence when she saw Nash sitting at the table. With eyes wide, she did her best to recover, but it was obvious she was rattled by his presence. Nash didn't blame her. The last time she'd seen him she'd been shot at and nearly died. He'd reluctantly killed the assassins, an act no civilian should ever be forced to witness. Doing the only thing he could think of, Nash gave her an apologetic wave. She blushingly waved back before turning her attention to preparing cutlery for the evening's dinner rush.

Returning to the table, Paul caught the exchange. "Wasn't she the waitress the night you met Tartarus?"

"Good memory."

"MI6 don't pay me for my pretty face." Paul set down the beers.

"Thank Christ for that."

They both chuckled, and for a moment Nash forgot the troubles of the world. It was unfortunate how fleeting that moment was.

Nash asked, "How's Nancy doing with all this? It has to

be tough on her. This isn't her bag, and she's been dragged away from everything she knows."

Taking a contemplative sip, Paul said, "This is going to sound odd, but I think this has been good for us."

"That does sound odd."

"We'd both been so occupied with our own careers, moving house and everything else life throws at you, we'd neglected us. This kind of forced us together—no, that's the wrong word. It *brought* us together without distraction, and we reconnected. It's been amazing."

"You've been having loads of sex is what you're saying?"

"Not *just* that." Paul hid his amusement behind his pint glass. "But yes, quite a bit of that too." Raising an eyebrow, he asked, "Speaking of, what's the deal with you and Sophia? You seem chummy again. I always said you were an idiot for letting her go."

Paul knew all about Nash's history with Sophia and had even run interference when MI6 raised concerns about a member of their esteemed organisation being in a relationship with someone from the DGSE. He'd made their concerns disappear, an act Nash was forever thankful for.

"To be honest, I'm not entirely sure." Nash took a sip of his Newcastle Brown and waited an appropriate amount of time before adding, "By the way, she told me we have a daughter."

Paul performed a spit-take worthy of a silent movie star. "You fucking what?"

Amused at his friend's reaction, Nash filled him in. Oddly, the more people he told, the more used to the idea he became. The two kicked the subject around for a while, Paul asking countless questions. There seemed to be a topic Paul was itching to discuss but was reluctant to do so.

Taking the news onboard, Paul leaned forward. "Do me a favour, would you?"

"Anything."

"Promise to be a better father than the shitemonsters we called dad, yeah?"

Nash lifted his glass. "I'll do my best."

Paul's face didn't reflect the humour of Nash's. "I said promise, not say you'll try." Paul gripped his arm. "I've known you long enough to know that when you promise, you keep your word or die trying. Promise me or don't, just don't bullshit me."

"I promise, Paul."

"Jesus," Paul waved a dismissive hand, "don't get all mushy."

Nash laughed, something that had been a rarity of late. It was a nice moment. It didn't last. Paul turned suddenly serious.

"Is this plan of yours going to work?"

"It has to, doesn't it?"

Before he could answer, the rest of their ragtag team surged through the doors. And what a team it was Eva, Bishop, Nancy, Harry, Sophia and Hawk. In spite of the circumstances, Nash's heart surged with affection for his friends. They all represented different aspects of his life and he would gladly give his life for any of them.

The sudden arrival of so many bodies invigorated the pub. The camaraderie and playful needling provided an energy that had been absent mere moments before. Sophia in particular took in the surrounds. She appeared to like what she saw.

The group arranged themselves, moving tables together to accommodate their number. Bishop with his plaster cast and crutches was placed at the end of the table. Eva manoeuvred herself next to him, ever ready to assist in any way she could. Whether by design or fluke, Sophia sat next to Nash. Further rounds were bought and in no time they were acting like a rowdy group of friends instead of an elite selection of trained professionals on the eve of the most important mission of their lives.

Lila came to take their dinner orders and was far more relaxed than when Nash had first seen her. Hawk's presence helped, as he was a known local and engaged in familiar chit-chat, putting her more at ease.

After she'd left and the group broke off into their own side conversations, Nash gently touched Sophia's arm.

"I would very much like to meet Sabine."

"I'd like that too." Her smile was as wide as it was warm. "But you'll need to survive this first."

Nash's features softened. "I'll do my best."

"You'd better." She took a sip of her wine. "This is a beautiful town. I could see myself retiring here."

Not for the first time, Nash wondered what it would be like to settle down with Sophia. When they'd been dating it was always a nice daydream stifled by their careers. For the first time, it felt like it could be real.

As if reading his mind, Sophia asked, "Do you think it was all worth it? The sacrifices we made, the loneliness of the roles we'd chosen? The countless things we were forced to surrender for king and country? Did we make the right choices?"

"I used to think yes," Nash said honestly. "I retired with every confidence I'd done the right thing, that I'd made a difference."

"And now?"

"I don't know. I really don't."

"What don't you know?" Eva turned, joining their

conversation. "I mean, there's so much you're completely ignorant on, but what are we talking about right now?"

Nash chuckled and filled her in.

Squashing her face, Eva groaned. "That's bollocks and you know it." Seeing the scepticism on Nash's face, she added, "Don't look at me like I'm a walking cum rag. You've saved countless lives, shaped the world for the better. You've improved the world far more than most mouth-breathing bell-ends who use words like irregardless, aksed and expresso."

Nash snorted. "You have the most eloquent way with words."

"Fucken A, cunt."

"Could you be more Australian?"

"I could pull a kangaroo out of my arse?"

Sophia let loose a full-bellied laugh that lifted the entire table. "Eva, I absolutely love your take on life."

Eva beamed. "When this is all over, we're definitely partying hard in London." She snuck a sideways glance in Nash's direction. "We'll even bring grandpa along."

Sophia giggled. "You'd be surprised how hard this one can party, believe me."

Seeming impressed, Eva accepted the comment without question.

"Tell me, Eva. When this is all done, will you and Bishop be going back to MI6?"

Eva blinked several times, contemplating her response. "Huh. You know, in all this time I never really thought there was any other option but returning." She absentmindedly glanced at Bishop's immobile legs and then turned back to Sophia. "I... I'll need to give that one a bit of thought." Pensiveness crossed her face like an eclipse. "Actually, a lot of thought."

She turned to Bishop and the two leaned in close and engaged in an intimate exchange for some time. Nash had to wonder what exactly they were talking about.

At the end of the table, Nancy tapped the side of her water glass with a knife to garner everyone's attention. "So, those who know Paul and me know we've been trying for a kid for some time now."

Eva dropped her glass on the floor and her hand darted to her mouth. "Oh, my dog."

Nancy went on, rubbing her belly as she did. "Paul and I are having a little sprog."

The table erupted in shouts of congratulations, hugs, back slapping and handshakes. Eva was the first to scoop her bestie up and the two cry-laughed while dancing in a little circle. Bishop hobbled up and clinched both Paul and Nancy together in a fierce bear hug. Despite having just met, Sophia and Nancy embraced as old friends, rocking from side to side in mutual excitement. In was a bliss bomb in a time of high anxiety, and a most welcome one.

So *that* was what Paul had wanted to tell him earlier. Nash was so happy for his friends, yet at the same time, a little sad. Paul and Nancy would raise their little one in a loving environment, yet Nash had missed out on ten years of Sabine's life. There was nothing he could do to change that now, though. He recalled his promise to Paul not to be a wayward father. He just had to survive the next forty-eight hours.

To lighten his own mood, Nash was about to ask Hawk to regale them with a story from his treasure-trove of colourful SAS yarns when his phone beeped. Glancing down at the screen, he instantly scooped it up and began reading.

Noting his change in mood, Sophia asked, "What's going on?"

Tapping the table to get everyone's attention, Nash said, "Sorry to interrupt." He held his phone aloft. "Cavendish has responded. He's acknowledged my email and wished me well. We all know what that really means." He lowered his head. "They'll be coming for me."

Without another word being spoken, everyone at the table downed the remnants of their drinks and stood. Every one of them had their game faces on. They were ready. They had to be.

The devil was coming to Devil's End.

FOURTEEN

"Are we a hundred per cent sure he'll be coming in person?" Nancy asked as they gathered around the architect's table at the centre of St. Stephen's Abbey. It was presently being renovated and the inside had been almost completely gutted, hence the drafting table, piles of yet-to-be-erected scaffolding, welding gear, paint tins and folded drop sheets.

On the table was a map of the village, strategically covered with military markings and notes. It was essentially a battle plan, covering as many contingencies and strategies they could collectively conceive.

"Knowing him as I do," Paul replied evenly, "he isn't going to leave this to chance. That's why we sent the email when we did. We knew it coincided with Cavendish's departure from New York." Nash noticed that Paul had stopped using the word "father". "He has a meeting with MI6 in two days' time and he's a man who doesn't want loose ends. He'll want Nash eliminated before the meeting and, being who he is, there's no way he's going to leave the operation to chance. Given his own organisation lied to him about eliminating Pinchot, he'll want to see Nash dead with his own eyes."

"Uh, great," Nash replied. "I think."

"That's why he'll want to oversee it in person." Paul seemed to be thinking it through as he spoke. "He'll leave nothing to chance. He'll be here. That's why we need to be ready."

Nancy seemed a little taken aback. Nash understood why. She wasn't used to Paul's business manner. To her, he'd always been the affable, somewhat daft, lovable husband. She'd only just discovered his position within MI6 and had never seen him in business mode. She appeared impressed.

Harry munched on a protein bar. "What about Pinchot?"

"What about him?" Nash asked.

"Isn't he another loose end?" She shrugged. "He's been part of this from the beginning."

"He may swing by," Nash said casually.

"What? Why?"

"There was a reason I sent the email unencrypted." He grabbed a protein bar for himself. "Pinchot was obviously privy to Cavendish's communications or he'd never have known Cavendish would be in New York. That was up-to-date intelligence he shouldn't have had access to once he'd been thrown out of Tartarus. I'm betting he's already on his way, just like Cavendish."

"Isn't there a chance he'll mess things up?"

Nash eyed Hawk. "We have contingencies in place for that."

The entire group had spent the night going over their detailed plans. Everyone contributed suggestions or posed pertinent challenging questions. Even Nancy and Harry, who weren't experienced espionage agents, came up with useful ideas. It was certainly a team effort.

Not knowing how much time they had certainly challenged them, but everything was falling into place. Well, almost everything.

"Not wanting to be that guy," Bishop pronounced, "but we seem to be severely lacking in the weapons department." He hobbled closer to the table and put his crutches to the side. "I for one don't want to take on whatever Cavendish is going to throw at us with two starter's pistols and a packet of Walkers Cheese and Onion crisps."

"I'd murder a packet right now." Eva rubbed her stomach. "Actually, I'm famished."

"I believe we have ammunitions covered." Nash turned to Hawk. "You want to do the honours?"

"Thought you'd never ask."

With a flourish, the bald Scotsman removed a dusty drop sheet to reveal armaments worthy of a small army. There were collective gasps all round, followed by several impressed whistles. Once again, Hawk had come through. During the satellite phone call, Nash had provided him with precise instructions to locate Nash's hidden treasure on the grounds of his old family estate. It contained heavy armaments and ammunition as well as a cache of silver and gold, which Nash advised Hawk to use to buy everything else on his extensive list. Hawk had his own stash and had contributed to the haul. In fact, it was his old mentor who provided the inspiration for Nash's own hoard.

The armaments contained a collection of KS1 Carbine rifles, G17 pistols, boxes and boxes of ammunition, a stash of grenades. Nash noted a few additions Hawk hadn't mentioned.

Bishop reeled in surprise. "Bloody hell, is that a L2A1 ILAW?"

The man was right. The L2A1 ILAW was an unguided anti-armour rocket launcher designed to be carried by a single British soldier. It wasn't something one expected to come across on an empty stomach.

Nash leaned over to Hawk. "One day you're going to tell me the story of how you came across that."

Hawk rocked on his heels. "I simply forgot to return this baby when I retired. Must be getting forgetful in my old age."

"That's a hell of a thing to forget," Bishop observed.

"In my experience," Hawk rubbed his beard, "one never wants to be caught short in a firefight."

"There's a difference between being caught short and annihilating the opposition."

In a steely tone, Hawk replied, "I fail to see the distinction."

Bishop beamed. "I'm not arguing with him."

"Wise man," Nash conceded.

There was a lot of lethal firepower on the table, all of which Nash hoped would be redundant, but he couldn't be sure. He'd created a plan that would hopefully result in minimal casualties, but there were no guarantees. Should things go badly and his team need protection, the weapons were there, but he hoped it wouldn't come to that. Nash had to conceded there was a lot of hoping and wishing involved in his plan, far more than he'd like.

Nancy elbowed her husband. "Do you have a stash like this in our back shed?"

"Only a couple of Challenger 2 tanks. Nothing to worry about, my love."

Giving her husband a side-eye, Nancy replied, "In the

past I would have thought you were joking. Now I'm not so sure."

Nash picked up a box of pistols, extracted one and stripped it down to its components in seconds, laying the pieces on the table. "This is a standard issue self-loading, semi-automatic, short recoil, locked breech, tilting barrel pistol. The G17 is made with a high-strength nylon-based polymer created by Glock which increases durability. You'll all be drilling with these until they become part of your body."

Harry raised her hand. "All of us?"

"All of you, yes."

Harry beamed. "Smashing."

"Almost all." Eva was uncustomarily sheepish. "I've had a chat to Nance, and given her current medical condition of sperm poisoning—"

"Ewww."

"— she, Paul and I have agreed she needs to get the fuck off the battlefield." She turned to her friend. "I'm going to miss seeing the Irish hellhound kicking arse and taking names, but none of us could live with ourselves if anything happened to little Eva."

Nancy twisted her mouth to the side. "I'm not naming this sprog after you, you Aussie tart."

The two shared a hug.

Nancy went on. "Normally, I'd fight to stay no matter what."

"You, fight?" Eva said mockingly. "What?"

Nancy rubbed her tummy. "But it's no longer just about me."

Nash was relieved. It was one less conversation he had to have. This was no place for a civilian, let alone a pregnant one. At least Harry was familiar with firearms and had been in her share of scrapes. This was all new to Nancy, and as much as he was growing to know her and thoroughly enjoyed her company, she couldn't be here when her father-in-law arrived with guns blazing.

After tearful farewells and a lot of hugging, Nancy left and promised to return following a definite victory or meet the team at their designated fallback position. It was heartening to see the love between Paul and Nancy. It almost brought Nash to tears himself. The two were so opposite, yet so thoroughly suited to one another. When she'd left, Nash took Paul aside and threw his arm around the tall man.

"You'll see her soon."

"I know." Paul sniffed. "But it rips my heart out that she has to go because of my own damn father. Like that son-of-a-bitch hasn't fucked up my life enough already."

"We do this right, he won't be causing you grief ever again."

Paul slapped his hands together. "Well, let's bloody get to it then."

HARRY'S ACCESS to Tartarus had been severed. The hacked IT credentials no longer enabled her free rein in Tartarus's servers. In the absence of that goldmine of information, they'd pulled together a status through a combination of trustworthy MI6 and DGSE contacts and media coverage following The Vessel attack. Cavendish was making his play for acceptability. A report in *The New York Times* was the first to announce to the wider world the existence of Tartarus, stating that they'd tried to warn authorities of the imminent terrorist attack in New York but had been dismissed.

There was some fluff about Cavendish himself, the former head of MI6 bringing knowledge, freedom and lollipops to the world. The report stopped short of offering a glowing endorsement, however, expressing concern at the susceptibility of a private spy agency to the whims of its leadership and noting how quickly good intentions—in theory, of course—could be warped into self-interest and manipulated to serve the agenda of the highest bidder.

Nash suspected Cavendish would be seething that the impact of aborted The Vessel attack wasn't as intended, because the waters had been muddied by the actions of Nash, Bishop and Eva. Although their claimed innocence had been well and truly brought into question after their dramatic escape from police custody.

Sophia was advised by several trusted contacts within the DGSE that Cavendish's push for Tartarus to have a seat at the table was gaining traction there. As far as she could tell, at least three of Five Eyes' countries had reached out for preliminary talks, MI6 included. The fact that the meeting in a day's time was with the heads of MI6 and the Foreign Secretary meant he clearly had some leverage. Cavendish could very well be winning. It stood to reason he had to eliminate Nash and his team to ensure his ascension wasn't hindered by something as inconvenient as the truth.

Nash paced around the map of Devil's End they had drawn on a large drop sheet on the floor of the abbey. Paint tins, paint brushes and pieces of masonry represented the parts of the village most relevant to the plan. A toolbox in the centre represented the abbey itself, which would be their communications centre and first fallback if things didn't exactly go to plan.

He strode over to Harry, who had created a makeshift table and chairs from painters' planks and empty paint tubs. She was huddled over her laptop.

"How are you holding up, Harry?"

"Fine, fine." She was distracted by her screen.

"You know you don't have to be here? This isn't your fight."

Now he had her full attention. Nash wasn't sure he wanted it.

"And you know you can shove a cactus up your arsehole sideways." Her upturned lips betrayed her true feelings. "I've been your man in the chair from the start, that's not going to change now. You can't get rid of me that easily."

"If you're sure?"

"I am."

"Then we're lucky to have you."

"Yeah, you fucken' are." She chuckled and asked, "How'd you guys get this place?"

"The abbey? The restoration is being done with the local university, and with the students away for February break nobody will be back for at least two weeks."

Hawk strode over with cheer in his voice. "All set for the cars. You should have seen the bloke's eyes light up when I offered him one of your gold sovereign coins."

"Nice work. Could you help Harry here with the comms check?"

"It would be my pleasure." He gave Harry a dazzling display of his pearly whites. "What can I do to assist such a capable and handsome woman?"

"Smooth." She gave a good-natured chuckle. "You sure you're this idiot's friend?"

Hawk slapped his big hand across Nash's back. "Most assuredly."

It wasn't the first time Nash thought he'd detected a hint of flirtatiousness between the two. He left them to it, whatever *it* was.

On the other side of the vast space, Paul, Bishop and Eva worked on their own projects. Paul coordinated their collective efforts with a combination of words of encouragement and jokes to lift the others' spirits. Even from across the space, Nash could see the bond between them. Sure, they were friends, but it was more than that. They shared a well-honed respect forged in the fires of battle, sometimes literally. Paul had been their superior, Nash's too, but he had never acted like it. He was the glue that bound them all together.

Paul was next to a half-built scaffold, working head down on his project while Eva and Bishop completed theirs. As Nash approached, Paul let out a cry, then cradled his thumb as he tossed away a hammer. He'd been cutting car tyres into long strips and hammering in large nails. Nash checked out his handiwork.

Lifting one, he assessed the heft. "You need more weights at the end of these. When they're used, you won't have time to hope they land the right way up. They need to drop into place instantly."

Paul shook out his hand. "On it. There are some brake pads over there, I can stitch them into the ends."

"Perfect." Placing his hand on Paul's shoulder, Nash asked, "How you holding up?"

"Fine."

"Your thumb says otherwise."

Paul gave a bow of his head, conceding the point. "I'm better knowing Nance is safe, but I want to be here, I *need* to be here. I need to set things right." He inhaled and composed himself. "Plus, why would I miss what is destined to be one of the greatest battles in history? Up there with the likes of the Carthaginians versus the Romans, the Greeks versus the Persians, Blur versus Oasis. How could I miss that?"

Nash ignored the forced bravado. "You're not responsible for the sins of your father."

"Perhaps not. But I will be responsible for stopping him."

"You don't have to be here."

Paul locked him with a steadfast glare. "Yes, I do."

Not wanting to argue, Nash gave him a friendly punch on the arm, then moved towards Eva, who stood over white buckets, stirring the contents with a broom handle while wearing a respirator, hazard gear and goggles.

"How goes the chemical mixing?"

Eva removed the respirator and wiped her hands on a rag. "Fine. And by fine, I mean I passed out twice and I'm pretty sure I'll be blind by forty, but it's done."

Nash placed his hand on her arm. "Are you really okay?"

"Yeah, just being dramatic." She gave him a soft smile and then hoisted her thumb at the buckets she'd been mixing. "This is some serious shit you boys managed to get. You didn't pick all of it up at Homebase, I know that much. Care to share how you happened to get your hands on it?"

Nash raised an eyebrow. "I got the habit from Hawk, actually. He's like an extreme Boy Scout, be prepared and all that. I had the gold stashed away for an emergency, though this wasn't on the list of possibilities I had at the time. Most of the chemicals are actually pretty widely available. Industrial cleaning, pool maintenance—hell, bread manufacturing. You just need to know the recipe."

"Uh, not everything is freely available."

Nash held a finger in agreement. "The fentanyl, Hawk

had to, ah, acquire from a less than reputable associate—you're right, that's not something you can buy over the counter at Boots." Nash noted Eva's incredulity. "The guns and weaponry were all contingency stuff accumulated over years, all of it before I chose the non-violent path. Then one day it was too late to hand it back, so I kind of left it. I never actually thought I'd need it. You know me, I always try to keep out of trouble."

Eva nudged him. "The only problem is, you're very, very bad at it."

He scratched the back of his neck. "Don't I know it."

Nash moved on to check on Bishop. With his crutches propped against the chair next to him, he was busying himself loading clips and carrying out an inventory of weaponry, noting details on a clipboard as he went.

Seeing Nash approach, he said, "I want to do more. I feel completely superfluous here."

"You should be resting, not racing around preparing for an attack. You only just escaped hospital."

"I'd still prefer to be out in the field when this thing happens than stuck half a mile away from the action." Bishop's expression softened. "Can I ask you something?"

"Always."

Bishop pointed to Nash's wrist and lowered his voice. "You traded your vintage Rolex for a phone call. You're churning through your gold reserves paying for all this. You're using yourself as bait for a man who has demonstrated repeatedly that lives mean nothing if they stand in the way of what he wants." He leaned back. "You're not planning on surviving this, are you?" Receiving no answer, he went on. "I've been on what I thought were one-way missions before. There's always another way. We're all here to keep one another safe, Mason. That includes you."

Nash thought it was the first time Bishop had ever used his first name. "I want to survive this."

"I can't help thinking there's a missing 'but' at the end of that sentence."

"But it has to end here. No matter the cost."

Bishop folded his arms. "Well, then let's make sure we prevail."

"Let's."

Once everyone had finished their tasks, Nash called them to the centre of the room where the impromptu map of the village was laid out. He went through the plan again, calling on each of them to advise what occurred next. Each of them would play a critical role in the success of the plan.

After completing the second run-through, Bishop pointed to a side street with his crutch. "I think this is a better funnel point. Huckleberry Lane gives them Bryerland Road to sidestep into and regroup. That could be seconds we don't want to give them. Ermin Court siphons them into a dead-end straight away. It'll remove any possibility of retreat and make them panic."

"They're going to be hardened mercenaries," Eva observed. "They're not likely to panic quickly."

Nash gave Hawk a sideways glance. "Oh, we'll panic them."

"We sure we can evacuate the village in time?" Sophia asked.

"The immediate town's population is only eighty-seven," Nash replied. "By our estimations it could be evacuated in less than an hour. Half of them will probably be at the pub anyway."

Sophia acknowledged the response but appeared far from convinced. She was the least onboard with their plan. Nash thought it was because she hadn't seen what every member of the team was capable of. He had, and he had enough faith for them both.

They ran through the plan another two times, each member adding their own ideas, which only strengthened the overall plan. They were as ready as they were going to be.

Calling for a break, they all sat or munched on stale sandwiches. It was past dinner time, but Nash were too hyped for food now. They were all on edge, but focused. Nash was certain he'd never worked with a better set of individuals.

At her improvised desk, Harry was immersed in whatever was on the screen. She'd hacked into traffic cameras controlled by Highways England, the government company charged with running England's motorways, and overlaid a facial recognition program to flag Cavendish in a car. Nash guessed her focus indicated something had happened.

"Positive ID?"

Harry squinted at the screen, clicking on various things. "Not exactly."

"Well then?" Nash was confused.

"See these gits?" Harry pointed to the screen, where a set of three black Land Rovers sped down the M40.

"I can see the cars but not the drivers."

"Tinted windows."

Nash shook his head, not understanding.

Harry grunted in frustration. "Okay, unless Led Zeppelin are playing Chipping Norton, these bastards are standing out like a collection of skeezy sore thumbs. They could have piled into a few Ford Fiestas, but no, they had to go all Marvel movie bad guy obvious."

"You're sure it's them?"

"As sure as I can be." She scratched her chin. "They're

186

headed straight here, at exactly one kilometre an hour below the speed limit. No deviations, no popping into a Starbucks for a coffee-like drink and a slice of carrot cake."

"Fuck Starbucks!" Eva cried out, specks of sandwich flying from her mouth.

Harry chuckled and continued. "These guys are the shit and they're coming straight for us."

"Good enough for me. When will they get here?"

"Best guess, around ten. Park, have a stretch and a scratch, be ready by, say, midnight. Your assessment of the wee small hours was spot on."

Nash took a wide stance, mind racing, already moving on to the next conversation. "Hawk!" When his old friend came over, Nash said, "It's time to evacuate."

"On it." His hand delved into his pocket to extract his keys. "I'll get the truck. Bishop, you make the call."

"Affirmative," Bishop replied, picking up his phone.

Phase one played out according to plan. Hawk jumped in his truck and headed into the village. At a designated corner he hit the brakes, strategically dislodging barrels covered with scary biohazard stickers, which proceeded to roll down the street.

Bishop called the police, stating in his best Cotswold accent that a biological hazard had just occurred with drums containing vinyl chloride, class-three dangerous goods due to their flammability. Bishop said the drums appeared undamaged but were "very scary". It was important to advise that the drums were undamaged because any real leakage would necessitate a full-blown emergency response with dozens of agencies, putting even more people in the firing line.

Given the notice of the fast moving SUVs heading their way, Nash and his team were cutting it fine, but they didn't want civilians wandering around and becoming collateral damage in their little war. The less people hurt the better. He only wished the opposition shared his outlook.

Luckily, the local constabulary followed protocol and activated a precautionary evacuation of Devil's End. Every available police officer was deployed to assist with the evacuation. They followed the regimented procedure and contacted the Hazardous Area Response Team. Except, they didn't. Harry rerouted the call to her mobile and advised a team was en route. Enter phase two.

Nash and Sophia drove in a van emblazoned with the official Hazardous Area Response Team logos. They wore matching overalls with printed logos Nash had also paid for. All the rushed jobs Hawk organised had cost Nash a small fortune, but the results spoke for themselves.

At the main entry to the town, the one connected to the M40, was positioned a rather rotund senior officer and a bookish policewoman. As soon as the van rolled to a stop Nash and Sophia and stepped out, and the two police at the roadblock straightened to attention. Nash did the talking, thinking Sophia's accent would only raise questions. Both officers seemed pleased to have HART on the job, grateful they didn't have to do the dirty work.

It tuned out the local police were surprisingly competent. They covered the two entry and exit points to the village and cleared it in less than an hour. Nash was quietly impressed. No locals put up a fight, and they were calmly evacuated to nearby Kingham. Apparently some were quite happy to be put up for the night.

"How long is this going to take?" was the first thing the Senior Sergeant asked.

Nash looked over to Sophia, who gave a theatrical shake

of her head. "From the briefing we received, a good five to eight hours."

The Senior Sergeant's shoulders sagged. "Our shift ended three hours ago." The black bags under his eyes reinforced his point.

Doing his best to give an air of sympathy, Nash said, "Look, we've got two more vans on the way. Trainers and students in their last semester. All fully qualified in road management. We can take over the outer cordon as we'll have too many for the hot zone anyway. Happy to do it."

"Really?" The Senior Sergeant's mood softened. "It's just, it's my husband's birthday and..."

Nash held up his hand. "Say no more. You go, we've got this. All good." He gave a reassuring wink. "When we're done we'll put the barricades on the side of the road over there. You can collect them in the morning. We got ya."

"That's brilliant, thank you so much," he called over his shoulder. He and the policewoman were already halfway to their car.

As their taillights disappeared into the night, Nash and Sophia quickly moved the barricade to the side of the road, careful to conceal it from view. They didn't want anything to prevent Tartarus from entering their trap.

Nash pulled out his comms device. "Phase two complete."

"Not before time," Harry replied anxiously, "they're about five miles out." She was stationed on the roof of the abbey, as it had the best view of all entry points. "I've got a visual. Better get out of there, Nash." There was a dramatic pause. "Here they come."

CHAPTER

FIFTEEN

The moment Nash parked the van, now stripped of its Hazardous Area Response Team logos, at the corner of the T-intersection, Bishop barked in the comms device in his ear.

"The Land Rovers have entered the town." There was a slight pause. "They've split up. First team heading directly for Nash's house, second team holding back."

Damn. They'd hoped Tartarus would stay together, but suspected they wouldn't be that lucky and had planned accordingly.

Nash and Sophia were positioned down the street and around the corner, but they had a good vantage point for what was about to unfold. Sophia extracted her pistol and rubbed his back reassuringly.

Nash hit the comms button. "Plan Omega. Repeat, plan Omega. You ready Paul?"

"Call me Mr Sandman."

"I'd rather not."

A dry chuckle came through Nash's earpiece. "Ready."

After a moment of silence, Paul said, "I have visual. Here we go."

Nash saw the SUV cut its headlights and roll to a stop four houses away. Five mercenaries in full tactical combat gear silently exited the van, carbines up and scanning for threats. They covered every direction in a wedge fire-team formation and silently slid through Nash's front gate. The dark-clad figures descended on the house, two heading towards the back door to cover any attempted escape.

It was textbook execution. These guys were pros. Nash expected nothing less.

From the way each of the team members moved, he was sure Cavendish wasn't among them. They were too fit and fast to be the older man. Nash only hoped his nemesis was in the secondary group holding back.

"Hold, Paul."

Paul was stationed inside Nash's house, awaiting the violent incursion. In a hushed voice, he replied, "Holding."

Using a breaching ram, the lead mercenary smashed into the front door. Instead of the old wooden door splintering into a thousand pieces, it held firm. Second and third attempts garnered equally unimpressive results. The lead mercenary shook his sore arms and turned to his team, issuing orders.

Nash turned to Sophia and grinned. "Had it reinforced years ago."

Returning his amusement, she asked, "I thought you were retired?"

"I was, but I'm also not an idiot." He raised an amused eyebrow. "You make some enemies in the espionage game."

"Obviously," Sophia responded with a smirk, still observing the unfolding scene.

A second mercenary stepped forward with a breaching

shotgun and blew out the hinges. The blast echoed through the still night. A similar explosion was heard from the other side of the house, no doubt the back door being breached.

"Subtle these guys aren't," Nash observed. More to himself, he added, "They're going for speed over stealth."

"That means they're being reckless." Sophia's features grew serious in the moonlight. "It means they're more dangerous."

Nash watched the last of the team storm into what had once been his quiet little sanctuary. "Let's do something to lessen that, shall we?" He pressed the talk button. "Paul, hit it."

There was no immediate response. Not via comms, nor any obvious activity inside Nash's house. The following seconds were among the longest of Nash's entire life.

"Paul, status?"

Receiving no response, Nash stood to rush to Paul's aid. Sophia gripped his arm and shook her head. They'd discussed this. If Plan Omega went sideways there would be no rushing in to save his friend because it would already be too late.

Time ground on and Nash's heart was in his throat. Had everything fallen apart already?

The silence of the country village was as oppressive as it was terrifying. At least they hadn't heard gunfire, but that didn't mean Paul was safe. *What the hell is happening?*

"Gas," Sophia stated quietly. "I see gas."

She was right. A white vapour billowed out through the demolished front door, noiselessly rising into the cold night. Nothing happened for several more glacial seconds.

Finally, a tall lanky figure slouched through the front door. Clad in black, the man's head was encased in a large gas mask. Once clear of the gaseous substance now seeping from Nash's house, he removed the mask and sucked in the night air deeply, like a drowning man taking his first gulp of precious oxygen.

Fiddling with his ear, Paul's voice came through Nash's earpiece clearly. "Result." There was clear relief in his voice. "Sorry, when I put on the mask I knocked out my earpiece. They're sleeping like babies."

Nash had gotten the idea from an old Spetsnaz operation. In 2002, Chechen terrorists had stormed a theatre in Moscow. The FSB team had pumped a gas known as M-99 into the ventilation system to incapacitate the terrorists. Unfortunately, the results of the raid had been less than stellar, with many of the hostages dying. Hawk and Nash had created their own home-grown version of what had been used that day, a fentanyl-based compound capable of rendering anyone unconscious in a matter of seconds. In the small confines of Nash's house, the risk was far less than in a huge theatre. The concoction Eva had mixed had done the trick.

Nash and Sophia donned their own masks and followed Paul back into the house. They stripped the Tartarus team of all weapons, tossing them into a large plastic tub Nash had used to store his winter coats. They bound their captives' hands and feet with FlexiCuffs. They also opened all the windows and doors so the fentanyl-based mixture would dissipate and not cause respiratory issues, a major reason for the failure of the Spetsnaz assault.

Paul, Nash and Sophia made their way outside and called in the success of the third phase. In a matter of minutes, half of Tartarus's team had been taken out of the game. More importantly for Nash, no one had died. He knew the next phase would not be as clean.

"What's the status of the second set of Land Rovers?" Nash asked.

"Same position," Bishop replied. "Likely shitting their pants now that they're receiving dead air from their... hold up. They're moving. Heading south to your position. Phase three in play. Repeat, phase three in play. You ready Eva?"

"Affirmative. In position. Team Spikey One ready. You ready, Team Spikey Two?"

Nash broke into a jog, Sophia close behind. "We're not calling ourselves Team Spikey."

"Yeah, we are." Eva waited a moment. "They've rounded the corner. Paul just joined me."

Breathless, Paul replied, "In position and in desperate need of some cardio training when this is all over."

"Sophia and I are in position," Nash said.

"I bet."

Nobody replied to Eva's snide comment. Crouching behind a brick fence in a neighbour's front yard, Nash didn't dare glance at Sophia next to him.

Nash was concerned they hadn't had a visual on Cavendish yet. He wasn't one of the unconscious Tartarus team on the floor of his lounge room. He could be in one of the approaching SUVs, but that was an assumption. Without capturing him, this whole operation would be for nothing.

Nash sucked in a lungful of air and waited. It was all he could do.

Hitting the comms button, Nash asked, "You ready Hawk?"

"When haven't I been ready?"

"Tanzania."

"That was once, and they were twins."

Not wanting to tie up the channel, Nash chose not to

answer. Sophia gave him an amused, quizzical look. He replied with a look of his own: *I'll tell you later.*

Hawk came on the line again. "Visual. They're turning into Ermin Court. Going silent. Heads up everyone. We've got this."

Seconds later, Nash saw them too. Two Land Rovers, headlights off, crept down the road. Nash hadn't known it was possible for a SUV to appear sketchy, but here was his proof. The two vehicles travelled at around five miles an hour, as if scared something would leap out at them. They were right to be cautious.

No doubt the occupants of the vehicles were concerned that every member of the breaching team went silent at the same time. *Surely one of them should have raised an alarm if the raid had gone wrong? All their comms gear wouldn't have failed at the same time, surely? They were here to take out one man, how could he take down six of their highly experienced mercenaries simultaneously?* They were no doubt spooked.

The rear SUV slowed to a halt at the entrance of the court, while the lead vehicle crept forward. This wasn't what they wanted. Both vehicles had to be in their trap before they could spring it.

The first Land Rover crawled slowly forward, while the second remained stationary, its engine still running.

"Move, you bastard," Harry growled through Nash's earpiece. "Move."

"Stow the chatter."

"Affirmative."

The first vehicle parked behind the Land Rover used by the breaching team and stopped directly in front of Nash's house. No one exited the vehicle. It was like they were debating what to do next.

Slowly, the furthest SUV finally moved towards the first. Collective sighs of relief came through the team's earpieces.

"Hawk," Nash whispered, "light 'em up."

"Already ahead of you, partner." There was a variety of clattering sounds followed by a *woof*. "Fireworks incoming. Team Spikey, you're on."

"Fuck yeah, Team Spikey!" Eva yelped.

The two teams leapt into action. Targeting the lead Land Rover, Nash crouched and ran towards the front of the car and threw one of their homemade spike strips. Made from old tyres, they were studded with nails and screws. Nash laid his in front, Sophia at the rear. Paul and Eva did the same to the rear SUV.

As they laid their trap, the sky above the far end of the court burst into an intense orange. A burning Vauxhall Cavalier rolled across the intersection the rear Land Rover had just passed. The flames and thick choking smoke reached high into the cold black sky. The bonfire on wheels crashed to a halt on the kerb, the burning old rust bucket blocking any escape for Tartarus' mercenaries.

The results were as predicted: the drivers of the respective vehicles panicked. Both threw their cars into reverse, their tyres screeching as they frantically backed up. Almost instantly, their rear tyres blew out. The rear SUV braked, the front vehicle didn't, crashing into it. The move also pushed both vehicles over the next spike strip, taking out all of the tyres.

Nash, Sophia, Paul, Eva and Hawk surrounded the Land Rovers, aiming carbines at the windows. Each stood with steely cold expressions. In the space of a few minutes they had incapacitated the breaching team and now held the second team at bay.

Nash yelled at the crashed vehicles. "Stand down! No

one needs to get hurt today. You will all be unharmed. This is your one chance. Stand down, now!"

They had the advantage, the firepower and the tactics and, more importantly for Nash, not a single life had been lost yet. Everyone held their breath. He stole a glance at Sophia. Her face was ice-cold determination and he didn't think he'd ever seen her look more beautiful.

"Nash..."

Harry's voice interrupted in his earpiece. He ignored it.

From inside the first SUV a voice shouted, "Fuck your offer!"

Sophia shouted back, "Is that a no?"

"Nash..." Harry repeated.

Whispering to Sophia, but on the open comms channel, Nash asked, "They're cornered. What are they holding on for?"

"I know," Harry replied, exasperated. "Nash, that's what I've been trying to tell you. There's another Land Rover en route. It's not fucking around, they're motoring."

Sophia nudged him with her elbow. "Cavendish."

"Why do you say that?"

She frowned. "Let the first two teams get their hands bloodied and he comes in to confirm the kill and hide the evidence. It fits his MO."

The woman has a point.

"They've hit the village limit and..." Harry hesitated. "What the hell?"

Nash pushed the earpiece further into his ear. "What is it?"

"There's another car," Harry said, "a sports car of some description..."

Bishop cut in. "A Ferrari LaFerrari if I'm not mistaken. It —woah, it just smashed through the barricade at the northern entry point. The driver's a maniac on a mission, wherever he's going."

Nash highly suspected where the car was headed, and who was at the wheel. "Looks like the gang's all here."

They hadn't exactly planned for this eventuality, but Nash knew his team was up for the challenge. Right now, he had more pressing matters.

Stepping forward, he pointed his carbine skyward. Sophia joined him, but her weapon wasn't as non-threatening. Eva, Paul and Hawk held firm, aiming their weapons at the rear SUV.

Nash shouted, "Will you stand down? No one needs to get hurt today."

For the longest time, no reply came from the SUVs. Nash hoped to hell that meant Tartarus knew they'd been outmanoeuvred. He wanted them to surrender peacefully.

They did not.

The front windscreen of the lead SUV shattered as a burst of machine gun fire exploded from the front seat. Sophia reacted in an instant, returning fire. She pushed her knee into the back of Nash's, grabbed the back of his tactical vest and pulled him to the ground. The response from the rest of his team was as rapid as it was brutal. Hawk, Eva and Paul strafed the front vehicle with gunfire. Within seconds the front Tartarus SUV was no longer firing. The engine of the wreck of a car spluttered and clunked to a wheezy end. No windows remained intact. It more closely resembled a cheese grater than a means of conveyance.

"You okay?" Sophia asked nervously.

Brushing himself off and pushing himself up, Nash replied, "Lead free, thanks to you."

The rear Land Rover's front door clicked open and all weapons swivelled in its direction. The second tense standoff was shorter than the first. A multicoloured leaflet of some description was waved above the roof.

"Sorry, we don't have a white flag."

At least Nash's plea for non-violence had appealed to some of the Tartarus mercenaries. *But not enough,* Nash lamented.

Hawk shouted, "Open the front passenger window and toss out all weapons. Now!"

He spoke with such authority, Nash was half inclined to throw his carbine down himself. Instead, he moved towards the first decimated vehicle. Every window was blown out, the three bodies—two in the front, one in the back—were bloodily pulverised and were virtually unrecognisable as human. The gruesome bullet-ridden forms reminded him more of Halloween mannequins than men.

"Fuck." He shook his head, crestfallen. "This is what I wanted to avoid at all costs."

Sophia placed her hand on his shoulder. "I know."

Even in their minced form, the men in the decimated Land Rover were too bulked up to be Cavendish. Sophia had called it. He must be on his way in the second wave, having lost comms with his teams.

The four surrendered Tartarus mercenaries were escorted to Nash's house by Hawk, Eva and Paul and promptly tied up with their compatriots.

On his return, Paul was smiling. "Some of those gents are positively chatty. They've got some stories to tell, more than we know, even. All we need to do is win this thing and they'll issue statements, I'm sure of it."

"Good to kno—"

Across comms, Bishop cut Nash short. "Ferrari's hit the centre of town, and... huh, it just stopped. Someone's getting... Visual confirmed, it is Pinchot. He's headed to your twenty. The Rover's... shit." He paused. "They've turned up McClintock. They're headed right for us. They're heading to the abbey."

Eva came on comms. "Get out of there, Bishop!"

"I'll try, but running isn't exactly my forte at the moment."

"I'll get him out," Harry advised firmly.

In his mind, Nash reassessed the changing battlefield. They'd won the first two skirmishes but were no closer to their objective. They were now planning on the fly, a situation that never made him comfortable. He was reminded of the quote from German military strategist Helmuth von Moltke: no battle plan survives contact with the enemy.

"Right," Nash said with more authority than he felt, "Eva, Hawk, you take on Pinchot. Sophia, hold position in case they send anyone else to the house, but don't take any risks. Paul and I will back up Harry and Bishop and face Cavendish."

Eva stepped forward, eyes wild. "But Bishop's my—"

"That's exactly why I'm going. And that's why you're going after Pinchot. He has a way of getting under my skin, every time. He'll expect me to confront him, he'll even take pleasure in it. I won't give him the satisfaction."

Not waiting for further argument, Nash slung an extra carbine over his shoulder and picked up a pump action shotgun the Tartarus mercenaries had discarded. When he straightened up Sophia was before him, her eyes focused but soft.

Her voice was low. "I've just found you again, I don't want to—"

"We've got a date, remember?" He kissed her gently on

the lips. "I'm coming to France to meet Sabine. You're not getting rid of me so easily."

She attempted to arrange her features into something resembling reassurance, but only partially pulled it off. Turning to Eva, Nash gave her an encouraging wink.

"You get him back."

He held the side of Eva's face. "I'll get him back, Eva, I promise."

Paul and Nash sprinted towards St. Stephen's Abbey on the hill. The Benedictine structure was visible from most of the village, which made it the perfect vantage point, but also a hell of a thing to get to in a hurry.

The black sky was pockmarked with tiny stars, and the new moon offered little illumination. It was a dark night for dark deeds.

"We're not going to make it in time." Paul's long legs raced up the steep grass incline.

"I know, but we have to try." Nash didn't take his eyes off the target.

Even with his long stride, Paul started to fall behind. He was inhaling heavily. "You shouldn't have promised Eva."

Nash gritted his teeth. "I know."

"A commander can't promise everyone comes home. You know that better than most."

"I said I know, Paul."

Nash was puffing now. The hill was hard going, but knowing what was about to unfold, he pushed through it.

"This is all my fault."

Nash spared a moment to shoot his friend a glance. "We've gone through this, Paul. We're not responsible for the sins of our fathers. All we can do is live a better life, do the best we can, otherwise we live in their shadow."

"But if I'd only I'd—"

"There's no way you could have foreseen this. No one could. This isn't your fault."

"Then why does it feel like it is?"

Unable to answer, Nash powered on. He slowed slightly to allow Paul to stay with him. He'd need the backup.

Between progressively louder pants, Paul asked, "How did Pinchot get here?"

"I don't know. He could have followed us or Tartarus, tapped into our comms or theirs." He shook his head. "It doesn't matter, he's here and now things are a lot more complicated." Flicking the comms switch, Nash addressed the team he was racing towards. "Bishop, sitrep."

In a hushed voice he replied, "We lost visual when they—"

A burst of gunfire cut Bishop off. Short eruptions of automatic fire were interspersed with grunting and gasps. It sounded like a running gun battle, the team engaging with the enemy intermingled with Harry declaring, "Fuck, fuck, fuck, fuck."

Nash and Paul sprinted as fast as their tired legs could propel them. They were still not over the rise, the full view of the abbey concealed behind the grass horizon.

There was more gunfire, followed by unintelligible shouting, rustling and indistinct thumps. Nash could hear clear footsteps and a crackling sound. It was followed by an eerie silence.

"Nash?" The voice was as calm as a frozen lake. "You there, Nash?"

There was no mistaking the self-assured voice. Nash and Paul slowed to a halt at the top of the hill and waited a moment to catch their breath. They hadn't made it in time. They'd lost.

Gripping his carbine tight, Nash hit talk on his comms. "I'm here, Cavendish. If you hurt my people—"

"The time for childish threats is over." He waited, no doubt relishing his position. "This petty vendetta you have ends now. You will come to the abbey and we'll end this. There's no need for more bloodshed."

If Cavendish was asking Nash to come to the abbey, that meant he didn't know he was already there. They might have a chance of surprise, but it would be momentary. Nash took his finger off comms to think for a moment.

"You know, if this was a movie, this would be where I say it's a trap, right?" Despite the words, there was no humour in Paul's tone.

"Oh, I know."

Nash took in the scene. They were twenty metres from the abbey, its windows dark, except for computers, a few lights they'd rigged to illuminate battle plans and a few kerosene lanterns in case the power failed. Nash and Paul stood behind the large oak front door at the main entrance of St. Stephen's, an empty black Land Rover parked haphazardly across the front steps.

Below them, the quaint little village of Devil's End hardly looked like its ancient earth had been tarnished by blood this night. It was more a picture postcard than a location of deadly skirmishes. *Not that there's such a thing as postcards anymore,* Nash reminded himself.

He checked his weapons; Paul followed suit. They hadn't verbalised a plan as yet, mainly because they didn't have one.

"Come on Nash!" Cavendish bellowed triumphantly in Nash's earpiece. "Just you and me. Let's have at it. Only one of us is leaving here tonight."

With no visual inside, Nash had no way of knowing if

Harry and Bishop were alive or dead. His optimism hoped for the former, his well-honed cynicism leant towards the latter. The individual inside was responsible for so much death, so much misery. The architect of Tartarus and its evil conniving ways. Behind the heavy double wooden doors was the way to end it once and for all. Removing Cavendish would mean an end to Tartarus. An end to running. An end to more deaths. It just required a sacrifice.

Nash rested the shotgun in the crook of his arm and hit talk on his comms. "Cavendish, you once said your theory about me was once a killer, always a killer. Maybe you're right." He turned to Paul. "Let's end this."

Once Nash released the talk button, Paul said, "You'll die."

Giving a nonchalant jiggle of his shoulders, Nash replied, "If I don't go in there everyone will."

Paul shook his head. "No, I'll go. This is my responsibility. *He's* my responsibility. He won't kill his own son."

"Are you sure?"

"No. But I stand a better chance of surviving than you do."

"I can't ask you to do that."

"I know. That's why I'm going."

"Bless you Paul, but you've never been in the field. You're not trained for this, I am. Whatever happens in there, it needs an experienced hand, and as much as I love you, my friend, that's not you."

"But your vow of non-violence—" Paul's fortitude was wavering, but he valiantly persevered.

"Every rule has an exception. I hope not to exercise that exception, but if I have to..."

Paul frowned. "You do what you have to. I'll do the same."

The men shook hands. It felt like a farewell.

From inside the abbey, more shots were fired. A woman screamed.

Nash straightened his back. "They may be the most powerful private secret agency in the world, killing everything we hold dear, but there's one thing Tartarus never counted on."

"What's that?"

Nash pumped the slide of the shotgun. "An old man with a shotgun."

He took a step into the light.

"That's a hell of a last line," Paul observed.

"I don't intend it to be." Nash mentally readied himself for what was to come.

"Neither do I," Paul replied with surprising resoluteness. "This is my fight."

"What does that—"

Nash didn't see the blow coming. For an office manager, Paul could land a decent punch. The pain in the back of Nash's skull flashed through the rest of his body in an instant. Years of painful experience had showed Nash he could take a blow, but the crack on the back of his head sent him crashing to the ground, his vision blurring around the edges. The last thing he saw before everything went black was Paul striding towards the abbey's doors.

CHAPTER
SIXTEEN

When Nash came to he had no idea how much time had passed. Seconds? Hours?

Using every ounce of strength he could muster, he pushed himself onto all fours. The exertion felt like climbing a mountain. Vision blurring, he used the shotgun as a crutch to propel himself upright and staggered unsteadily towards the abbey.

Touching his right ear, he realised his earpiece had been dislodged when Paul knocked him out. He repositioned it and switched to the alternate frequency.

"You there? It's Nash."

"Nash!" Eva replied. "What happened? You've been off air for two minutes, we were getting worried."

That answered the time question. He quickly brought the others up to speed. "Sitrep?"

"He's gone," Sophia said flatly.

"Who's gone?"

"Pinchot." Hawk's tone was as brusque as Sophia's. "He baited us. Enticed us to run to the centre of town and when we were close, he took off in his sports car. No idea where he is now."

That complicated matters, but he couldn't focus on Pinchot right now. He needed to get inside and rescue his friends. Before what would likely be his final act, he had to get the others to coordinate their efforts so they could finish this if he couldn't.

"We need to find Pinchot." Nash eyed the abbey, scanning for any movement.

"No need," said a voice behind Nash, "I'm right here."

Nash spun around. In the half-light, Pinchot's grotesque scarred face beamed behind the business end of a Negev NG-7 that was pointed directly at Nash's heart.

His eyes were wilder than Nash had ever seen them, and that was saying a lot. Pinchot was hopped up on something, perhaps everything.

"Drop the shotgun," he growled.

"Sure thing, Pinchot."

The name drop was for his compatriots down the hill in the centre of the village.

"He in there?" Pinchot asked, jerking his head towards the abbey.

"Yes, but don't go in, my people are in there. I don't know what the situation is."

"Then you're not a very good spy, are you?"

"There have been complications."

"Life's like that, isn't it?" Pinchot's manic wide mouth made him look more like an animated villain than a human being.

"Nash, can you stall him until we get there?" Eva's voice was strained, she was running.

Looking into Pinchot's manic dilated pupils, Nash replied, "I highly doubt it."

Stepping forward, Pinchot took Nash's shotgun and the

two pistols in his holsters. He then yanked out his earpiece, pulling the wire out completely. Nash was cut off, with only a madman for company.

"Let's go pay Pops a visit, shall we?"

"I can handle this, Jack. They're my people in there and I need to—"

"Enough of your goody two shoes bullshit!" Pinchot screamed. "This ends here and it ends now."

Manhandling Nash towards the entrance, Pinchot kept his enemy in front of him at all times. When they reached the entrance, he thumped the huge double doors with the butt of the shotgun. As the echoes reverberated inside, Nash watched the American's hands. They were shaking. He was barely holding himself together.

"Cavendish!" Pinchot shouted to the heavens. "It's your protégé coming back to the fold. I just want to talk. You owe me that much, old man!"

Quietly, Nash said, "If you're trying to appeal to Cavendish's better nature I have bad news for you."

Ignoring him, Pinchot screamed, "Come out here you evil cunt. I've got a score to settle."

Nash didn't expect a reply, and wasn't surprised when one wasn't forthcoming. "I don't think that's going to entice him out if I'm being completely honest."

Faint footsteps echoed from the interior of the abbey, followed by clanks and sliding metal bolts. The main door creaked open a crack to reveal a silver-haired mercenary.

A burly voice from inside said, "Drop your weapons and you can come inside."

From the delivery, he sounded ex-military. Perhaps an ex-cop.

"Acceptable."

The burly man said, "Drop the Negev and open your jacket."

Pinchot let his Negev fall from his hands and opened his jacket, gently removing a pistol from his holster. An ex-cop wouldn't have stopped there. The guy behind the door did.

The door opened wider to reveal a huge bulk of a man with a slab of meat for a head and no discernible neck. He flicked his gun at Nash, indicating that he should do the same. Once satisfied, he opened the door fully and patted each of them down before ushering them into the dark confines of the abbey.

Inside the dimly lit interior, Nash quickly took in the situation. He decided to call the slab of a man who'd let them in André the Giant. André lumbered over to join his Tartarus compatriot, who Nash labelled Junkyard Dog. The two had the room covered. André aimed his carbine at Pinchot and Nash while Junkyard aimed his at Harry and Bishop. Harry was visibly scared, a rare condition for the formidable woman. Bishop nursed a bloody blow to the head but appeared otherwise unscathed.

Paul stood next to his father at the old altar. Hatred bled off both men. André motioned with the barrel of his gun for Nash and Pinchot to step forward. Nash felt like he was being ushered to the altar to be sacrificed. It didn't exactly help that the flickering kerosene lamps gave everything a gothic edge.

The vast space was as Nash had left it. Various clumps of workers' materials throughout; a pile of paint tins here, a packing crate of plaster there, a few half-completed scaffolds in the corner.

As he drew near Paul, Nash gave his friend a sardonic nod. "Nice move with the coldcocking."

"The least I could do." Paul frowned. "I missed your birthday."

Nash turned to the other prisoners. "Alright, Harry?"

"Never better, Nash. I can't express how glad I am you got me embroiled in all this."

"Bishop, you alright?"

"Fine, fine." He took the handkerchief from his bleeding forehead and assessed it. "This is from my new mate over there," he waved it towards André, "who apparently doesn't take too kindly to a plaster leg to the goolies."

André grunted and took an angry step towards Bishop before being waved off by an annoyed Cavendish.

"That's enough banter, thank you."

Cavendish paced the raised platform like a British Raj. He could afford to be arrogant. He held all the cards.

Nash studied every face, every gesture, every outline of those in the room. He assessed their weaknesses, considered what their next moves could be. The last person he watched held a well-concealed ace. Strategizing how he could use it to his advantage, he was interrupted.

Cavendish slapped his hands together. "Well, isn't this fun? Together again."

With nothing left to lose, Nash thought he may as well kick things off and get it over with. "You've lost, Cavendish. Give up."

"Have I now, Mason?" Cavendish chortled. "From where I am, I'd say your little crusade is over once and for all." He folded his arms. "Too bad you won't live long enough to see the good Tartarus will do for the world, the benefit we'll bring to—"

Nash unleashed a thunderous groan. Swinging his head from side to side, he over-emphasised every word.

"Enough. With. The. Fucking. Sermons." He threw his hands in the air. "Every. Fucking. Time."

Pinchot crinkled his scarred forehead. "Are you trying to get shot in the face?"

Ignoring him, Nash went on. "It's boring, Cavendish. You're boring. You're a boring old twat who dresses like a banker from 1964."

Standing beside his father, Paul chuckled. His face suggested he suspected Nash was up to something, but didn't know what.

Nash continued as he rounded a packing crate piled high with plaster. "If you're going to kill me, do it now so I don't have to be subjected to another of your tedious rants about how Tartarus are a force for truth, justice and gold-plated cock rings everywhere. I just don't care. I don't." He stepped forward; André followed him with the carbine. "You're not building a legacy, you're destroying one—your own. You won't be remembered as the noble visionary who saved espionage for the twenty-first century, you'll be the man who brought down centuries-old institutions by infiltrating them with your own warped brand of evil. No one will thank you for that, they'll only revile you for it." Nash took two more steps, coming within metres of Cavendish. "You haven't saved MI6, you've condemned it."

In the corner, Bishop stretched his neck, seemingly cottoning on that Nash's rant had a purpose of some description.

Shaking his head in seemingly genuine confusion, Cavendish opened his mouth to rebuke Nash but was cut short when Pinchot pulled a Glock from his jacket and shot André between the eyes.

It was the gun André the Giant should have checked for when they'd entered the abbey, and now he paid the price for his sloppy work. Nash dove behind the plaster crate as bullets strafed the opposite side. Pinchot commando crawled beside him. With Pinchot armed, it was now two to one, slighter better odds than a few seconds before. Nash had noticed the outline of the gun under Pinchot's jacket when Cavendish had started monologuing, unsure how he'd managed to conceal it from André during the pat down.

Chancing a glance over the plaster, Nash saw Cavendish standing in the centre of the altar holding Paul in front of him, gun to his head. He was using his own son as a shield.

Nash's eyes darted to the pistol in Pinchot's hand. He wanted to wrestle the gun from him but wasn't certain he'd be able to disarm Pinchot without handing the farm to Cavendish. If the two fought and Nash lost it would be all over, and nothing but carnage on all sides.

Eva, Hawk and Sophia raced through the front doors of the abbey, quickly taking the situation in. Junkyard fired in their direction, but they managed to dive behind a large stone pillar.

The pendulum of odds had swung once more, but Nash and his team were far from a winning position. Hawk poked his head around the corner of the pillar and Nash gave him a thankful wave.

"Everyone stand down!" Cavendish's voice carried more command than he possessed. "I'll be leaving now, clear my way!"

"Give up, Dad. It's over. You've lost."

"Not when I'm this close." The man's voice was manic. "You'll see what we'll achieve. We're almost there. I won't be stopped by this pathetic rabble."

Beside Nash, Pinchot hyperventilated, his unhinged eyes as crazy as they'd been minutes before. The gun danced in his shaking hands. Nash had to wonder how he'd managed to take out André. Nash had learned long ago not to underestimate Pinchot, even in this dishevelled state.

"I'm here to kill you, Cavendish!"

"Really, I thought you were here to suck my cock."

Chancing a glance around the edge of the plaster again, Nash saw Junkyard frantically sweeping his carbine from side to side, eyes wide in panic. He'd taken his eyes off the captives behind him, more concerned with the armed newcomers.

Unlike Junkyard, Nash could see Bishop.

While Cavendish and Pinchot traded barbs, Bishop tore the plaster on one of his legs in two. He soon made light work of the second. Pushing himself upright, he stood on unsteady legs. Nash watched, open-mouthed, as Bishop took a step forward on what had very recently been two completely broken legs. Within striking distance, Bishop politely tapped Junkyard on the shoulder.

When he turned, Bishop landed a devastating right hook, but the force of the blow buckled his legs and both men tumbled. Not waiting to hit the ground, Bishop unleashed two more rapid punches to the man-mountain's head. Landing with skull-cracking force, Junkyard's head bounced up. Bishop screamed in pain but didn't let up. Grasping the strap of the carbine, he wrapped it around the big man's neck as his meaty hands desperately clutched at his smothered windpipe. In no time at all Junkyard stopped struggling and gave a final death rattle.

Now it was just Cavendish. Nash turned to his right and corrected himself. Cavendish and Pinchot.

"Jack. This is over. You just need to—"

Pinchot leapt to his feet, aiming his pistol at Cavendish. In reply, the ex-director of MI6 staggered backwards, his son positioned in front of him, gun to his head. As he did, Cavendish knocked the architect's table Nash's team had been using as a laptop charging station. The bump dislodged a kerosene lamp, which landed on a pile of painter's tarps that was soon engulfed in flames.

"I'm walking out of here!" Cavendish announced, his head twisting to catch sight of the missing Junkyard, not having seen him fall. When Hawk, Eva and Sophia emerged with newfound confidence, he screamed, "Get out of my way!"

"Dad, it's over."

"Shut up! Shut up!"

In a low voice, Nash addressed Pinchot. "Put down your gun, Jack. We can resolve this. He has nowhere to go."

"Never." Pinchot spat the word like venom. "Not after what he's taken from me."

Cavendish's glacial movement towards the exit was steady. Paul's footing faltered, but his father held firm and half dragged, half guided his hostage on.

"You're not leaving, you son of a bitch!"

"Jack, stand down." Nash dared raise his voice at the deranged man.

"No!" Pinchot swung his weapon towards Nash, warning him to stay back. "I won't let him win."

"He won't. We can stop him, but you need to give me the gun."

"You little goody-two-shoes losers will arrest him. He needs to *die*."

Closer to the door, Cavendish was heading towards Eva, Hawk and Sophia. Nash waved for them to move out of the way.

"No!" Pinchot broke into a run.

"Jack, stop!" He turned to Bishop. "Take him."

Bishop awkwardly aimed his carbine, but his legs beneath him weren't stable. He fired. He missed.

Pinchot ran at the retreating Cavendish. The old man glanced over his shoulder, saw the threat and opened fire. Pinchot returned in kind and the two exchanged volleys. Bullets flew in all directions. Paul stumbled and Cavendish sprinted alone towards the abbey's doors.

Nash picked up his discarded shotgun and swung it towards the sprinting Pinchot. Before he could fire, Pinchot reeled backwards, his chest an explosion of red. Nash's head snapped around and he saw Sophia in a firing stance.

"So you don't have to live with it." Sophia gave Nash a sad smile. "Plus, I owed him for Baptiste."

Eva screamed and dashed to where Paul had fallen. "No no no no no no."

Taking advantage of the chaos, Cavendish leapt through the door. Hawk and Sophia trained their weapons on a gurgling Pinchot, while Hawk kicked his pistol from his limp hand. Harry attended to the crumpled Bishop, his mangled legs finally given out.

Nash ran to Eva, who cradled Paul's head. As soon as Nash arrived by her side, he knew it was too late. Paul's eyes were open and their dead stare told Nash all he needed to know. He dropped the shotgun, his hands no longer functioning.

Tears streaming down her face, Eva caressed her friend's cheek. "Don't go, Pauly, don't go. We need you. Come back to us. Come back."

Her sobbing convulsed her entire body. She was inconsolable. Sophia appeared beside her and the two women embraced. Sophia gently eased Paul out of Eva's arms, placing him on the ground and covering his body with a tarpaulin.

Nash wasn't sure how he was still standing. His vision blurred. The world tilted on its axis. He wanted to throw up, to curl into a ball and never move again.

Paul, his saviour, his mentor and friend was dead. The man who connected them all, Eva, Bishop, Nash. The one who had led them all, had stood beside them when no one else would, had been slain. Paul Cavendish was dead.

Nash's lungs fought for air that didn't want to come. He felt like he was standing through some force unrelated to will. He honestly didn't know what to do. He was numb.

Hawk sidled up to Nash and shook his head at Pinchot. "Chest wound. He's a goner. Minutes at best."

Near the centre of the room, Harry and a wincing Bishop flung bottles of water at the growing flames. The fire had spread to the sheets covering the paint tins and showed no sign of abating. Nash had other priorities.

Hearing Hawk's words, no sadness reached Nash's heart for the man who had just killed one of the few friends he had on earth. All thoughts of compassion, of peaceful coexistence had been purged from his body.

With a rage he'd thought long quelled, Nash marched to the laying, gurgling Pinchot. He was thankful he had no weapon in his hand as he honestly didn't know what he would have done.

Somehow, Nash remained on mission. He had to, for Paul. He leaned down to Pinchot, whose blood dribbled from the sides of his mouth.

"You have more than one set of evidence against Cavendish and Tartarus, don't you?" Nash asked, somehow managing to unclench his jaw. "When you destroyed the laptop back in New York, that wasn't the only copy. Where is it?"

Pinchot coughed up blood. "I'm touched you care so much about my plight, Mason."

"You have nothing to lose now, Jack. You can manage one last act of selflessness. Where's the evidence against Tartarus?"

Pinchot wiped bubbling blood from his cheek. "I was only trying to do good, you know. I was trying to help."

"I know that's what you think."

"Then you forgive me?"

"No." Nash's word was a slab of ice. "You killed too many innocent people. You killed my friend. All I can do is understand, but I'll never forgive you."

Pinchot chuckled, but the effort caused him to wince in pain. "I admire your honesty, you sickeningly good son-of-a-bitch." He winced and coughed up more blood. He didn't have long. "Go to wheatusfans.org, you can access the back end with the username admin. The password is the first chorus of Teenage Dirtbag."

"Are you... are you serious?"

"I never joke about Wheatus." Pinchot convulsed, turned to his side and spat blood. "There's a whole mess of hidden files in there, your Harry will have no problem finding them. It has everything on the terrorist attack, the board, me, Cavendish, Tartarus, everything. You'll clear your names."

"I don't care about that."

"You should." Pinchot looked Nash in the eye. "You're a good man, Mason Nash."

His eyes glazed over and after a couple of deep inhales, drew air no more.

Jack Pinchot was dead.

Looking up at Hawk, Nash rummaged around in the pockets of Pinchot's jacket. "Did you hear what he said?"

"About Wheatus?" Hawk scratched the back of his head. "Yeah, but—"

Hawk stopped suddenly as Nash leapt up. "Help Bishop and Harry, the fire's getting out of control."

Without waiting for a reply, he ran for the door, pausing only to pick up one thing. Sophia was still consoling the weeping Eva and saw him running.

She called out, "Nash, stop. Wait."

Nash did not stop. He did not wait.

Holding the keys to Pinchot's Ferrari LaFerrari in one hand and a shotgun in the other, Nash sprinted outside. One friend was dead, but the information supplied by a dying Pinchot meant the rest of his friends would be safe.

Nash tossed the shotgun onto the passenger seat and started the Ferrari with a ferocious roar. Dropping the sportscar into gear, he spun the wheels and took off at speed. There was only one thing for him to do now. Nash was going to end this.

SEVENTEEN

Trees were a blur.

The Ferrari LaFerrari's hybrid V12 had a maximum speed of three hundred and fifty kilometres an hour. It was the fastest road car Ferrari had produced at the time. Nash was reasonably sure he could catch a Land Rover. The winding country roads wouldn't let him redline the beast of a car, but the way it hugged the curves allowed Nash to claw back the gap between him and Cavendish in no time at all. Within a minute he had the bastard in his sights.

Turning a corner near the Hangman's Inn, the Land Rover was pelting through the centre of the town, its driver desperate to leave, his plans for eliminating Nash in his home having fallen apart so dramatically. Cavendish would be frantic that his small army had been picked off one by one, leaving only their ruthless leader at large.

Not for long.

Nash took a racing line on the corner and threaded the Ferrari through the tiny gap. In seconds he was bearing down on the SUV. He didn't take his foot off the accelerator, which was flat on the floor. Nash saw Cavendish's head whip around as he heard the howling V12 coming at him like a bullet.

It was an apt simile.

The front bonnet of the Ferrari hit the rear right wheel of the Land Rover at ninety kilometres an hour. The shunt lifted the SUV into the air, sending it careening over and landing on its side. The impact deployed the Ferrari's multiple airbags and Nash's chest and arms were thumped with the protective devices as white powder impeded his vision. The Ferrari crashed to a halt.

Dazed for the second time that night, Nash staggered from the wreckage. The Land Rover was on its side, the front of the vehicle resting against the exterior wall of the pub. Cavendish shouldered the weight of the driver's side door slid against it's mass to squeeze out. He landed ingloriously on the asphalt with a *thud,* staggering away from the crash stunned.

Nash fired the shotgun into the air. That got Cavendish's attention. On the hill, St. Stephen's lit the night, the fire now visible through its stained-glass windows. The village was bathed in a haunting orange glow.

Cavendish stood with his hands in the air, although in one he held a pistol. He turned slowly to face his nemesis.

Nash pumped the slide of the shotgun and held it at hip height, aimed at Cavendish. "You killed your own son."

"I can still call the police, tell them you did it."

"My god, man, you're still trying to get out of this? Not even lamenting the death of your own child? You really are a psychopath."

"The police will believe me." Cavendish's arrogance was as steely as ever.

"No, they won't. We have Pinchot's evidence. All of it. He hated me, but he abhorred you even more. We have your men captive, some of whom have juicy stories they're willing to tell in exchange for immunity. You're cooked, Cavendish."

"I'll survive."

Never one to believe in clichés, Nash was surprised to find that his entire body felt like his blood was boiling. This man, *this bastard*, was utterly unmoved that Paul—his own flesh and blood—had died because of him. It took every ounce of strength not to pull the trigger in that instant.

The worst part was that Cavendish was likely right. Even with all of Pinchot's evidence, MI5 and MI6 would rather sweep it all under the carpet than face the ignominy of a trial where they would have to publicly admit how royally they'd fucked up. The esteemed and trusted former head of MI6 would likely escape the worst punishments; he'd get a light slap on the wrist at best. For all the death he had dished out, his own son included, he'd face little to no justice. Ramsay Cavendish would be a free man in no time.

Swallowing the bile that crept up the back of his throat, Nash lowered his head. "Did you know you were going to be a grandfather?"

"Wh... what?" Genuine surprise crossed his features.

"Nancy's pregnant. You just killed her husband and the father of your grandchild."

"Jesus." Cavendish shook his head. "I didn't mean for him to die."

"Using him as a human shield says otherwise, you son of a bitch."

Cavendish's gun hand drooped, but only for an instant. The steely take-no-bullshit visage soon returned. Nash could ask him to drop the gun, but they both knew he wouldn't. Cavendish would never concede a single advantage. It was how he was built.

Cavendish was responsible for the death of the man who'd saved Nash's life, who'd pulled him out of his downward spiral of a life without purpose. Paul had been a friend and mentor to Eva, Bishop, Nash and countless others. A good man lay dead while this human filth stood breathing free air. Christ, poor Nancy would never recover from this.

Seemingly reading Nash's mind, Cavendish lowered his gun and fired three shots, then kept pulling the trigger repeatedly. All three bullets missed their target and he had nothing left in the magazine.

Tossing the empty gun aside, Cavendish held his palms aloft. "You can't blame a man for trying." He lowered his gaze. "We both know you're not going to shoot me." The arrogance in his tone was nauseating. "Your pathetic pacifism won't let you, will it? You're a pitiful, wretched little man. Even now, even after all I've done, you can't pull the trigger." He let loose a delirious cackle. "The once great warrior, the scourge of evil empires everywhere is a frightened little coward. Drop the charade. Drag me to the authorities and let's see how that turns out for you."

"No."

"No?" Cavendish appeared genuinely surprised. "What do you mean, no? The famed peacenic Mason Nash is not going to shoot an unarmed man, no matter what I've done, surely?"

Nash sniffed and cracked his neck. "I don't know about that."

And then Mason Nash shot Ramsay Cavendish.

EPILOGUE

The sky was a remarkably clear blue for this time of year.

Nash dug his hands deep into the pockets of his long coat. The air had a chill, but there was the faintest hint of warmth which had been sorely missing for the last few months. The weather was finally looking up.

The lazy village streets were unchanged, in spite of Tartarus's best efforts. Repairs had begun a month ago on St. Stephen's on the hill. The inexplicable fire was blamed on careless workmen. The fact it had occurred the same night a biological hazard spill saw the town evacuated was put down to coincidence.

Life in Devil's End had returned to its natural state: slow moving and sedate. That suited Nash just fine. Making his way down the street in the warm afternoon sun, Nash was overcome with a sense of joy when he caught sight of the Hangman's Inn. The quaint pub had stood for hundreds of years and hopefully would for hundreds more, or at least until Nash was done with it.

Entering the low-ceilinged, near-empty pub, Nash gave

the publican a friendly wave. In return, she gave him a wink.

"Pint of Newcastle Brown?"

"You read my mind, Denise."

"That's my job, love."

Taking his usual position at the back of the pub, which afforded him the best view of every corner of the room, Nash nestled in and inhaled deeply. He'd learned to appreciate moments like this. Contented moments. There was a time not long ago when he'd thought he'd never experience them again, so he had chosen to appreciate them when he could. One never knew if they would come again.

"Dining alone, are we?"

Nash looked up to see Lila's pretty beaming face. It had taken some time, and a distinct lack of attacking assassins for her to become comfortable in his company again.

Nash returned the smile. "Not anymore, no."

Giving Nash a curious crinkle of her forehead, Lila left a pile of menus on the table and went to greet another local couple keen to spend the night in the warm confines of their local. Denise came by and delivered Nash's pint. He savoured that too.

After a few minutes later, Hawk entered and discarded his coat. He swung by the bar for a whiskey, then joined Nash at the table.

"Sorry to talk shop, but you okay to cover Kurt's English class on Wednesday afternoon? He's getting some dental work done."

"Sure, no problem."

The transition back to sedate teacher had been easier than Nash had anticipated. True to his word, Hawk had brought Nash back into the fold at his school. In no time at all Nash was issuing hall passes and marking homework.

The two talked shop and drank for a few minutes before the next group arrived. Eva was back to her natural raven locks, although Bishop still sported his ridiculous moustache, clinging to the inexplicable idea that he looked distinguished despite Eva and Nash's best efforts to dissuade him of the notion. Bishop held the door open to allow Nancy to roll the pram inside.

The group exchanged hugs and kisses and the room was soon overflowing with love and good cheer. Lifting her son from the pram, Nancy thrust the baby into Nash's arms.

"What am I supposed to do with this?"

"Hold him, you big eejit, what do you think? Mumma's got to go to the loo."

"Why me?" Nash asked good naturedly. It certainly wasn't the first time he'd held Nancy and Paul's child, and knew it wouldn't be the last.

"Because he's got your name, so one Mason can hold the other. At least until he needs his nappy changed." She gave Nash a kiss on the cheek and went with Eva to the bar.

Nash shouted to the departing women, "I thought you said you were going to the loo?"

Nancy gave a dismissive wave of her hand. "One thing at a time."

Holding little Mason in his lap, Nash saw the familiar facial features of Paul staring back at him. The little guy was only six months old, but he already looked like his father. And his height was in the 90th percentile, so he was already on the way to his dad's lankiness.

The loss of Paul had been hard on them all. The funeral was the toughest Nash had ever attended, and his eulogy left no dry eye in the church. There wasn't a day Nash didn't feel Paul's absence. The fact he'd been such a close friend to them all meant Nash was not alone in his grief.

Watching the two women chatting chummily at the bar, Nash nodded in their direction and addressed Bishop. "How's she doing, Nancy?"

Frowning, Bishop followed Nash's gaze then turned back. "Good days and bad, as you'd expect. She's one hell of a tough woman, that's for sure. She's got a lot of support. Eva's over there every day."

"You two still not back at MI6? It's been nearly a year."

The two spies, like the rest of their group, had been cleared thanks to Pinchot's evidence. The result had been explosive. Every major spy agency on the planet had been ripped apart by Pinchot's files. The public shitstorm had destroyed credibility in the once-revered organisations. In recent months the dust had begun to settle, but it would be a long time before the public's trust was restored.

Bishop gave a weary exhalation. "Even after we gave evidence we're not exactly the most popular folks in the halls of MI6 right now. Half hate our innards for bringing them into disrepute, the other half suspect we had something to do with it. So, no, we're not exactly rushing to get back. One day potentially, just not yet."

"Understandable." Nash took a sip of his beer.

"Plus, it won't be the same place we left, not without Paul." Bishop's eyes wandered to no particular point. "He was my manager for so long, and the only one Eva ever had. He was our mentor, but more importantly, he was our friend. The place won't be *our* MI6 without him, you know? Without Paul..." He shrugged.

Nash knew exactly what he meant. "What will you do until you decide?"

"Eva's got an old aunt who caught her on the media coverage and reached out. I think she mentioned her when we were in Melbourne. Nina used to be a scream queen in Hollywood back in the seventies, then a private detective. She's got some stories. We're going to hang out in LA with the movie stars and palm trees for a bit."

"Sounds terrible." Nash placed a hand on Bishop's shoulder. "You two deserve a break."

Bishop placed his hand over Nash's by way of thanks. The two had forged a tight friendship in recent months. Nash had come to relish their time together.

"Harry not joining us?" Bishop asked.

"Not today, she's up to her neck in the latest contract. She sends her regards."

When the full story of the small group's success became widely known, Harry had rightfully received praise for her tireless work. Job offers were showered on her by every agency with an acronym. While she said she'd never be a "suit", she was happy to accept ridiculous amounts cash for freelance work. Harry was even talking about retiring in a few short years.

Hawk leaned over. "I'm seeing Harry this weekend, I'll tell her you said hi, Bishop."

Nash and Bishop exchanged amused looks. Bishop in particular seemed to be sucking a particularly tasty boiled sweet.

"Will you now?" He leaned forward, placing his elbow on his knee. "Since when are you hanging out with Harry in London?"

Giving a blasé shrug, Hawk replied, "There's a new exhibition at the Tate we're both interested in."

Neither man believed him for a second, but they left it unchallenged. To save his friend further grilling, Nash changed the subject.

"Even after all these months I still find it funny Tartarus

227

were taken down by the band who released 'Teenage Dirt-bag'. I can't say I ever saw that coming."

"Who's coming?" Eva asked, returning to the table with a tray of shots.

Nash eyed the tray suspiciously. "Why are we doing shots, Eva?"

Before she could answer, the door opened and Sophia and Sabine walked in. Nash handed little Mason back to his mother, and another wave of hugs and kisses engulfed the table. The longest and most intimate kiss was reserved for Nash and Sophia.

"Ugh, get a room." Eva lips danced with amusement.

"I agree," Sabine said, disgusted as only an eleven-year-old could be.

Sophia and Sabine had been driving around looking at potential schools for Sabine. At the moment it was to be a trial six months to see how she'd settle into an English school.

The relationship between Nash and Sabine was growing. He'd be lying if he said he'd done everything right from the start, but this parenting thing was new to him. He was trying. Thankfully, Sabine was too. She was a bright and genuinely funny young woman who'd thankfully inherited her mother's cynical French sense of humour. The two had bonded over photography, Marx Brothers movies and a mutual love of tacos.

Sophia, on the other hand, required no effort whatsoever. The two had fallen in love all over again. They weren't the same people they'd been when they'd loved one another the first time, but their differences and experiences since then had somehow made them even more compatible. For a man so used to being a loner, Nash felt incomplete whenever Sophia wasn't with him. It had been her suggestion to trial Sabine's schooling in the UK. If it worked out, who knew what else would be possible?

"Hey, lady Sabine, how's the leg?" Eva asked.

Sabine had injured her knee falling from a tree stump while photographing the local countryside the week before. She and Eva had quickly bonded, the young woman fangirling whenever Eva was around.

"Good, thanks, Eva," she replied eagerly. "But, uh, why lady?"

Eva's head swivelled to Nash. "You haven't told her!"

"Told me what?"

"We were holding off on that," Nash replied.

"Holding off on what?"

Eva thumbed towards Nash. "Your dad's a lord, a proper one. That means you'll be a lady one day."

"What!" Sabine bounced in her seat. "Are you for real?"

"Thanks, Eva."

"Welcome."

While everyone sat around the long table exchanging stories and good humour, Nash stood back and savoured the moment. Perhaps for the first time in his life, he was truly content, truly happy.

Noticing his taciturn disposition, Sophia placed her hand on his sleeve. "Everything alright?"

"Yes," he leant in for a kiss, "everything is perfect."

His attention was once again drawn to the tray at the centre of the table. Nash asked, "Eva, what's with the shots?"

Eva tilted her head. "Didn't you see the news? Cavendish's trial ended today."

"No, I've been stuck in school play rehearsals all day." He clenched his fists. "What was the verdict?"

The press had labelled the prosecution of Ramsay

Cavendish as the trial of the century. But given that those seemed to happen every couple of years, Nash wasn't swayed by their bombast. It was certainly well covered. The prosecution had thrown everything at the man who had once been held in such high regard. The press did so love a tall poppy's fall.

Eva handed out shots. "They got him on nineteen of the twenty counts. The prosecution estimate at least two hundred years. That bastard isn't seeing daylight for the rest of his life."

Not replying immediately, Nash took in the news. He'd told his friends he'd contemplated murdering Cavendish with the shotgun, although he never fully explained how close he'd been to killing him. He was truly the most evil man Nash had ever encountered, and that was saying something. He'd been responsible for the death of Paul and countless others. Nash was sure Cavendish still walked with a limp where he'd shot him in the legs, a non-fatal, but still brutal blast. Nash was a good man, but not *that* good.

Unlike Cavendish, Nash had decided to trust in the very institutions Cavendish held in such contempt. He'd fought the violent urges and had stayed true to his own beliefs. Today, that decision had been vindicated.

Pushing himself up from the table, Nash walked across the room, everyone watching his movement. Once he reached the centre of the pub, Mason Nash proceeded to dance.

"What on earth are you doing?" Sophia stifled a laugh and shook her head. "Please stop."

Nash did not stop; he gave himself over to the moves. "It's the MC Hammer dance from 'U Can't Touch This'—what else would it be?"

"An epileptic fit?"

Sabine did her best to pretend to be embarrassed, although she too was laughing along with the rest of the table.

With hands on hips, Nash flicked his head from side to side as he executed his typewriter dance moves. "I promised Cavendish when he went down I would celebrate with this, and I'm nothing if not a man of my word."

Eva wiped a tear from her eye. "You might be a man of your word, but your dance moves leave a lot to be desired."

Puffing from the exertion, Nash said, "Either work hard or you might as well quit."

"I... I don't know what that means."

When Nash finished his victory dance, they all shared a shot to celebrate the demise of the once -powerful Cavendish. Sabine had to settle for a lemonade.

As the night wore on, more good cheer and stories were exchanged. Every so often Nash took a moment to appreciate what he had. There'd been times in the past when he would have thought he didn't deserve this level of happiness. He was glad he'd persevered. Before Tartarus he thought his best days were behind him, that he was an old man who would slowly wither away.

He'd been wrong. His life wasn't over. It was just beginning.

THE END

To be the first to find out when new novels arrive and to win prizes and get free stuff (who doesn't like free stuff?), sign up for my VIP Book Club at:
https://davesinclair.com.au/newsletter/

ACKNOWLEDGMENTS

What a ride!

This is the thirteenth book in what has been dubbed the Eva-verse – man, what fun I've had! Nash's story grew as I got to know him – I intended to kill him off when I first started the trilogy, but I couldn't do it! Sorry, Paul.

Is this the end of the Eva-verse??? Possibly? We'll see.

What's next? Well, those with an eagle eye may have spotted what's next in this very book! Stay tuned to see what comes from the writer's cave! https://davesinclair.com.au/newsletter/ for all the latest news!

And now - the acknowledgements!

First, and always is my amazing and beautiful wife Kristi. The engine behind my writing career and my first reader for everything. Monkey, heart, unicorn.

To my wonderful girls, Quinn and Esther, big embarrassing dad hugs!!! They always ask what I'm writing, love to see new covers and how I'm going. Big loves!

As always, to my tribe, the incredible G-Mob who are brilliant writers and even better friends. To Craig, Justin, Luke, Nathan, Kat, Joel, Amanda and Amanda, thank you for your support, encouragement and laughs.

A big up to my editor Vanessa Lanaway for making my words gooderer. Thank you!

Thanks to The Cover Collection who did a fantastic job on the covers for the whole series. I love the vibe and how they all come together so well.

Don't be afraid to reach out on Facebook, Instagram, carrier pigeon, mental telepathy. It's always great to hear from readers. You can stalk me at all these semi-reputable places:

www.davesinclair.com.au

https://facebook.com/DaveSinclairAuthor/

https://www.instagram.com/davesinclairauthor/

https://www.goodreads.com/author/show/22167525.Dave_Sinclair

https://www.bookbub.com/authors/dave-sinclair

If you can, please drop a review, it is greatly appreciated. It helps new people discover my work.

Thank you and here's to many more adventures!

Dave